MW01611591

The Northwoods Hymnal

The Northwoods Hymnal

First Edition: February 1st, 2013
All Rights Reserved.
Printed in the United States of America.

©2013, Stories: Luke Hawley
©2013, Cover Art: Holly Neeley
©2013, Music: Luke Hawley, Paul Dudrey, Joe Mann
©2013, Photograph of Luke Hawley: Sarah Hawley

ISBN: 9780983553045

Library of Congress Control Number: 2012947866

American Literature:

1   21st Century
2   Prose Fiction
3   Coming of Age
4   Individual Author, 2001 - Luke Hawley

Principal Editor: Diane Smith
Associate Editor: Joseph Michael Owens
Copy Editor: Tim Stobierski
Graphic Designer and Editor: Joshua Engen

All rights to *The Northwoods Hymnal* 2013 are reserved with River Otter Press. No part of this publication may be reproduced or distributed in any form by any means, or stored in a database or retrieval system, without the prior written consent of River Otter Press, including, but not limited to, any network or other electronic means of transmission, or broadcast for distance learning. ©Individual copyrights remain with the respective writers, artist, and photographers. River Otter Press consists of an all-volunteer staff.

River Otter Press
Po Box 211664
St. Paul, Minnesota 55118

The Northwoods Hymnal

by Luke Hawley

DEDICATION

For Sarah: I never would have written any of this
without you.

And to Eden and Judah: Thanks for taking long
naps,
among a million other things.

RIVER OTTER | *St. Paul, Minnesota*

CONTENTS

The Northwoods Hymnal

∞

Music was my refuge. I could crawl into the space between my notes and curl my back to loneliness.

—Maya Angelou,
Gather Together In My Name

Your Bones Get Old

Luke Hawley

Paul Dudrey

1. I knew a man spent half his life
2. I spend my days picking up the dead,

sel - ling in - surance in case of fire.
most of them dy - ing in their beds.

Some act of God to come cra - shing down
But no, not me, I will not go

burn - ing all his things into the ground,
Lying on my back waiting for Death to show.

Your Bones Get Old

When death came through he did not care,
I'll stretch my legs and split this town.

No insurance could save him from those stairs.
He can do his best to track me down.

Your bones get old before you know before you

know.
know, before you know

A Pretty Good Gig

"Hello," the old woman said, like a question, which he thought was strange because they should have told her that he was coming.

"Hi ma'am. My name is Hank. I'm from the coroner's office. I'm here to pick up..." He looked down at his clipboard for the name. "Mr. Galloway."

"Teddy," the old woman said.

"Yes." Hank tried never to be on a first name basis with the dead. "Can I come in the front door or is there a better way for me?"

"The front is fine." He could see her scalp through her white hair. He reached up and tousled his own mess.

He went back out to the van for the stretcher and made sure he had a fresh bag. The house was one of those places with a big open foyer and a high ceiling and a balcony overlooking the whole thing. A three-tiered chandelier hung from the middle of the ceiling. His eyes followed the staircase in a curve from the balcony down to the floor. At the bottom of the staircase was Mr. Galloway. Hank looked away, something he had never done before. But it was already in his head, like the moment after a flashbulb: Mr. Galloway in his robe and t-shirt and boxer shorts, not much more than a pile of white and blue and flesh. Hank was used to rolling bodies off of beds. But Mr. Galloway was something else. His arms and legs splayed in all directions. A piece of bone stuck out of his skin at the elbow. The doctor who pronounced him could have at least had the decency to straighten him out.

"Somebody's got to do it," Hank muttered.

He knelt over Mr. Galloway and unfolded the body like he was opening a piece of crumpled foil. He checked the pockets of the robe and, finding nothing, straightened him out the best he could. It was harder than he'd expected, and by the time he got the body onto the stretcher and headed toward the door, Mrs. Galloway had appeared.

"What do I do now?" she asked.

"I'll take him down to the funeral home and you can call down there and work out the details." The details meant the bill. He took a card out from his breast pocket and handed it to Mrs. Galloway. "Of course, you can call us if you have any questions. It's the number right there." He pointed at the number and looked at Mrs. Galloway. She offered a polite smile and he realized her question had nothing to do with who she ought to call.

Mrs. Galloway coughed. Hank thought it wouldn't be long before she joined her husband.

"Thank you, young man," she said.

He inched the stretcher toward the door, as close as he could get it. It felt weird to say you're welcome, but he did anyway.

"How did you get into this line of work?" she asked.

He should have just nodded and left. Now she thought he wanted to talk.

"Ad in the paper."

"My husband sold life insurance for forty-five years because of an ad in the paper," she said. "And it was good money."

"It's a pretty good gig, I guess." His words echoed off the high ceiling in the foyer and he watched to see if the sound would move the chandelier. From the corner of his eye, he saw her looking at him.

"I'll tell you God's honest truth. When he tripped on that stair up there he was probably thinking about insurance."

He thought about Mr. Galloway, running numbers in his head, thinking about annuity options and liability limits, missing the first step, teetering, tottering, losing his balance. A claim for every stair, all the way down, to the final company loss: death by foyer floor.

"I hear you, Mrs. Galloway. Last thing I want to think about in my last moment is all these bodies." She looked down at her hands and ran the thin skin over her almost-exposed veins. "Excuse me, ma'am," he blushed. "I didn't mean to sound so crass. What I mean is that I hear you and you're right." He opened the door to the house and pushed Mr. Galloway halfway out of his home.

"I'm glad to hear so, son. Your bones get old before you even know it."

"Yes ma'am. And thank you."

He pushed Mr. Galloway out to the van and put him in the back. He closed the back doors and walked around to the front of the van. Reaching through the open window, he grabbed a cigarette out of the pack on the dash. He watched Mrs. Galloway close the front door and pulled a pack of matches from his pocket and lit the cigarette, thinking about how empty that big house must feel. Maybe it was better to live alone in a little apartment his whole life. Except he couldn't play drums in a one-bedroom.

He ashed the cigarette on the grass next to the driveway, took another drag, and pulled a notebook out of his pocket. The cigarette hung between his lips, the way he had practiced when he started smoking. On the first blank page he wrote *before your bones get old*. Then he flipped to the back and jotted down some numbers, adding them together

and putting a box around the total. From his pocket
he pulled out a bank slip. In his head, he added the
total on the paper to the number on the bank slip.

∞

"I don't know, man." Hank set his phone in the
crease between his shoulder and ear and turned the
wheel right into the parking lot. "I'm still maybe a
hundred short." Something near the right tire
clicked, like baseball cards in bicycle spokes.
"Okay. Okay. Alright. Listen. I gotta go. I gotta run.
I'll call you later."

He hung up the phone as the sleigh bells
sounded against the store's door. The man behind
the counter smiled and pushed a few loose licorice
whips of black hair behind his ear. "Hammering
Hank! You here to finally buy those pearly whites?"

"Hey Willie."

"Best ballplayer I ever saw." Willie was over
stuffed and sloppy, a facsimile of his store. Hank
guessed Willie hadn't bought a new piece of
clothing in twenty years, though he wasn't diverting
wardrobe funds into the upkeep of his shop. "The
set's in back, same as always, but I gotta tell you
man, some guy in a tie came in today asking about
it. Something about his kid."

"Sure Willie. You and I both know none of
your customers wear ties."

Willie laughed. An exaggerated nod tossed his hair back over his ears to the front of his face.

Hank headed to the back of the store, tapping out ghost strokes on his jeans. It was a long rectangular room and the drums were in the back, past the wall of guitars and basses and the rows of amplifiers and cases of pedals. He sat down at the kit. Twenty-inch kick, sixteen on the floor, fourteen and twelve on the rack, all a glossy pearl white. A metal snare that would do the trick until he could upgrade to maple or walnut or something nice. A twenty-inch ride and two crashes, fourteen and sixteen. Hank pulled a pair of sticks from the bucket of try-me's.

He started slow, just single strokes on the snare, bringing in the kick on the quarters and the hi-hat on the eighths, finding a groove that he could sit down in. In a moment he was all swinging arms and legs, landing punches on every drum, hooks for the cymbals, jabs for the snare. He flailed, emptying the endorphins from his blood, stuffing chaos in a box of four-four bars.

When he was finished, he put the sticks back in the bucket and checked the tag on the drums. He grabbed the notebook and pencil from his pocket and chicken-scratched in the front, before flipping to the back and confirming his numbers. He stood up from the set and walked toward the front of the store. He inspected the wall of acoustic guitars, found one he liked, and pulled it down. The body had a dark tobacco stain and the finish had rubbed away in a couple of spots on the back of the neck. He sat on a stool and pulled the guitar close to him, putting his weight on the top of the body and letting it sink into his leg. He picked out the few chords he knew and hummed a simple melody.

∞

"Did you get the set?"

Dizzy was a living, breathing punk-star dream, black leather jacket and perpetual scowl. He spent what money he had on gear and cheap-looking clothes and he lived with his mother. Hank couldn't imagine still living with his folks, but Dizzy felt no shame. It stoked his megalomania—Dizzy saw himself as a tortured artist, under the buzz of fluorescent ballasts, surrounded by cement, a bare mattress, a tattered leather love seat.

Hank grabbed a beer from the small refrigerator dwarfed by a Marshall stack. He reached up to his ear and popped the ring out of the hole stretched in the lobe and pushed it against the cap to open the bottle. The beer was cold and flat. He checked for a date on the bottom of the bottle.

"Is your mom gonna let us play a full kit down here?" Hank countered.

Seth, the last limb of the band, snorted. He was sprawled out across the couch, extra long and lean, his bass up around his chin, wearing his usual plaid-print shirt. Hank recognized the changes from a Beatles' song ringing off the fat, unamped strings. Seth knew some things about music but he was quiet and no match for Dizzy's ferocity, so his opinions never got through his teeth.

"Shut up about my mom." Dizzy pointed a black-nailed finger at Hank. His hair jutted straight off his head, sharp stalagmites of gel and black dye. Hank had never seen it any other way. "Screw her anyway. I could find us a place if you get some drums."

Hank pulled the bottle out of his mouth and let it hang, just touching the edge of his bottom lip. "For free?" he asked, before tipping the bottle back.

"I don't know," scoffed Dizzy. "It's a mute point anyway."

"I think you mean moot," Seth said. He stopped playing for a moment and, using the knuckle of his thumb, pushed his glasses up his nose. He didn't wield his intelligence with spite; it was a fact he couldn't help.

"I know what I mean, dumbshit." Dizzy switched his amp on and stood up off his bed. "And quit playing that weakass pop music and plug yourself in."

Hank polished off the beer and pulled another from the fridge, before situating himself on the stool in the corner of the room. He pulled two sticks from his quiver and started hammering paradiddles on the practice pad in front of him. At his feet was a kick pedal attached to a Rubbermaid storage bin, to his right, a five-gallon bucket. He had ducktaped a tambourine to a lamp and a Christmas tin to a tripod for his hi-hat and crash. He tried once to convince Dizzy that it would be a perfect kit if they were going all out for noise rock, but at their only show it had been impossible to mic and his Christmas tin had come undone after a song and a half.

"Alright," Dizzy shouted over the din of warm up notes. "I got this new one I've been working on. Seth, it's pretty easy to follow, but Hank, I really need you to pay attention to the rhythm."

Hank held his sticks up, as if to say, What the hell else do you think I do? Then he said it. "What the hell else do you think I do?" He brought the sticks down on the head of the practice pad in rhythm with the storage bin at his foot: *Boom ClackClack. Boom ClackClack.*

"I don't know. But it sure seems like your head's not in the game tonight."

The rhythm was never the problem with Dizzy's songs. "Just play the damn song," Hank said. Dizzy strummed his pick over his single coil, holding his left hand loose against the strings. Over the racket of dead strings and feedback he shouted:

> *You don't know*
> *You don't know a thing about it*
> *You don't know a thing about me*
> *You don't know a thing*

Hank kept the quarter with the kick and watched Dizzy holler his way through the song. He rapped out a careful beat, four-on-the-floor, the snare on the three, the Christmas tin on the one and an occasional accented four. Seth stood, staring, not playing, watching Dizzy strum his dead strings.

The song finished in a hurricane of feedback and hum. Dizzy looked up from the microphone. "So? What do you think?"

Seth pulled his glasses off and held the frame between his index finger and thumb. He pushed his palms against his eyes, rubbing and groaning. "You didn't play any chords."

"I know, right?" Dizzy smiled, the gap from his missing eyetooth showing from behind his lower lip. "It's badass, isn't it?"

"It's stupid." Seth flipped the switch on his amp and pulled the chord out of his bass. Hank had never seen him move so fast.

"Where are you going?" Hank set his sticks on the practice pad and picked up his beer. He ran his left hand through his hair, pulling it into his fist again and again, and watched Seth open his case on the couch. They'd been meeting for over a year, putting together songs, and all of the sudden Seth had an opinion. A strong one.

"I'm out of here. This band is stupid. No chords?"

Dizzy flipped his amp to standby. "It's just something I'm trying out."

Seth shook his head. "No it's not. You can hardly play that thing." He waved the back of his hand at Dizzy's guitar. "You're trying to sell incompetency as novelty."

"Trying to what?"

Hank set the beer down and stretched his arm back over his head. Dizzy was heating up and he wanted to be ready.

"You heard me," Seth said. "Everything about you. It's all some silly act. Coolness over music."

"The music *is* cool. It's not one or the other. It's both. You're just stuck back fifty years ago. You can't hear the cutting edge."

Seth rolled his cable around his elbow and back over his thumb. "The cutting edge sounds like shit."

Hank laughed.

"What the hell are you laughing at?" Dizzy turned to face him. "You're the reason we suck."

"Don't turn this on me, Diz. I've offered to help write songs a hundred times."

"I don't need any of your help. The songs are great the way they are."

Seth tucked the coiled cable under the headstock of his bass, closed the case, and looked at Dizzy. "Tell me something, Dizzy. Do you really like sushi?"

"What?" Dizzy spun to face Seth. "What does sushi have to do with anything?"

"Just answer the question."

"Yeah." Dizzy widened his eyes and offered a slow, contemptuous nod. "I like sushi. So what?"

"Bullshit." Seth clicked the clasp closed on his case. "Nobody likes sushi. It's raw fish. It's terrible." He picked up the case and looked at Hank. "I'll see you around Hank. Good luck finding a set."

∞

Hank was picking up a couple of bodies at Ebenezer when he got the message from Dizzy.

"Dude. Find a way to get your kit. You have to. I got us a spot at Jack's."

He pushed the second body into the back of the van and weeded his smokes from his pocket. A tap on the pack and one slid out. He lit it and drew the notebook from his pocket, flipping to the back. He dragged the body back out and zipped down the bag. A guy in a bathrobe. That was no good. He zipped the bag up and shoved it back into the van.

Hank finished his cigarette and put it out on the heel of his boot. Ebenezer was a weird place to pick up because they didn't have a door in back like every other old folks' home. He had to park up front, in one of the handicapped spots. He couldn't imagine living in a home and having to watch Death, cloaked and scythed, walk in the front door every day. He thought of Mr. Galloway, crunching numbers in his head, then crumpled on the floor. And Mrs. Galloway, alone in the big empty house. Maybe it was better to watch Death come in and out than no one at all.

He slid the other body out. Slacks. That's probably what Mrs. Galloway would call them. He found a wallet and helped himself to the twenty in the crease. He pulled out his notebook and added the number to the page in the back.

"Still short," he whispered to himself. Then to the man in the bag: "But don't think I don't appreciate it."

∞

Jack's was packed. Hank elbowed his way through the crowd to the bar, where Dizzy was waving him over.

"This is great right?" Dizzy shouted over the mix blasting from the front of the bar. "What did I tell you?"

"Yeah." Hank flagged down the bartender. "The cheapest tap you've got."

"Four bucks."

"Four bucks?"

The bartender grabbed a glass and lifted it in Hank's direction.

"Okay. But it's robbery."

The bartender shrugged. Hank turned back to Dizzy. "Who are all these people here to see?"

Dizzy rolled his eyes. "Us, man!"

"Sure."

"Look. I don't know. But it's great, right?"

"Yeah. I think you already said that."

"What?" Dizzy shouted.

"Nothing. When do we play?"

"Not sure. They'll announce us."

"They'll announce us?" The bartender delivered the beer. Hank gave him a fiver and a shot of contempt. "How long's the set?"

"Two songs."

"Two songs?"

"What are you? A parrot?"

"Yeah." Hank gulped the top third of his beer. At least it wasn't stale. "There's got to be a hundred people in here."

"I know! It's great, right?"

"I'm the parrot?" Hank asked.

"What?" Dizzy shouted.

"Nothing." Hank scanned the crowd. It looked like every third person was holding a guitar. "How many bands are playing tonight?"

"What? I don't know."

"You don't know?"

"I said that, didn't I?"

A lanky, bespectacled man walked across the stage to the microphone. "How's everybody doing? I said *how's everybody doing*! Thanks for coming out to Jack's first ever open mic!"

Hank choked, but made sure to catch the beer in his cheeks and swallow it back down. "Are you kidding me? Are you kidding me, Diz?"

"What?"

"You said you got us a gig."

"I did get us a gig."

"This is an open mic. It is not a gig."

"It sure as hell is. There's over a hundred people here. What more do you want?"

"But you didn't get a gig. You put us on a list."

"A hard list to get on, man."

Hank watched as the first performer took the stage. He was wearing grandma glasses and holding a ukelele.

"Screw this. I'm outta here."

"What? No way, dude. You can't bail on me now! Don't be a douche like the bass player who shall not be named."

"Seth? He's just smarter than I am."

"He's a douche. Two songs. That's all. We're playing in the first half. They've even got a house kit for you. Just play the damn drums. Then you can go home and do whatever you do when you're at home. Finish your four dollar beer."

"Exactly why I'm leaving." Hank downed the last of his beer, set it back on the bar, and chinned at it. "Four bucks."

Dizzy grabbed his elbow. "Please, man. You've gotta stay. I'll buy you the next one."

Hank looked at Dizzy. "You'll buy me a beer? *You* will buy *me* a beer? Okay. I'll stay. Just for that." He looked up at the stage, where the man in the big glasses was finishing up his first tune. To laughter. "But we better play soon."

"Right on! I'll go talk to the guy about pushing us up." Dizzy smiled at Hank. "The things I do for your sorry ass." Hank watched as Dizzy disappeared into the crowd. He reappeared at the front of the stage, leaning in close to tell the MC something before backing out again to wave his arms around like a silverback gorilla. The guy nodded and Dizzy looked back at Hank, raising two thumbs high over the crowd. Hank rolled his eyes and made his way to the stage.

"Let's start with the new one. The one we worked on the other night."

"The one where you don't play any chords?" Hank positioned the snare between his knees. It was hard to get comfortable on a strange set.

"Exactly." Dizzy turned his volume knob all the way up and let the noise from his amp swell. "What's up everybody! We're Antithesis and we're here to rock!" He turned back around to face Hank. "Give me the first verse and then you come in right after that, alright?"

Dizzy strummed his pick against his deadened strings, his amp sounding a distorted *chicka-chicka*.

You don't know
You don't know a thing about it
You don't know a thing about me
You don't know a thing

"I know you suck!"

Hank heard the shout from the front row just as he came in with the kick and the crash. He dropped into his rhythm and watched through the space between the two cymbals as Dizzy swung the mic stand to the side and shouted into the front row. "You don't know shit about who sucks!" His amp

screeched and what crowd Hank could see covered
their ears. Hank stopped playing, letting the
cymbals fizzle out, but he couldn't hear anything
over the high-pitched guitar squawk. He saw The
Shouter in the front row give Dizzy the finger.
Dizzy continued to shout. The Shouter shouted
back. Something split the space between their faces,
traveling from Dizzy to The Shouter, and Hank
watched The Shouter go extra red-faced and wipe
his cheek off with his sleeve. The Shouter shouted
something more at Dizzy, who kicked wildly in
front of him, before slithering out from under his
guitar strap and leaping into the crowd. The amp
continued to scream as Dizzy landed two good
hooks on The Shouter before a couple guys from
the crowd pinned his arms back.

"You don't know a thing about anything!"
Dizzy continued his feral thrashing and The Shouter
backed away, clutching his face, bleeding. The
bartender made his way from the back and pointed
at the door, shouting. The crowd parted as Dizzy
was dragged out the fire exit to the left of the stage.
The heavy metal door slammed shut and Hank
realized he was standing alone on the stage in a
suddenly quiet bar.

"How about you drummer boy? You know how
to play?" Hank heard a voice in the crowd, but
couldn't see who it belonged to. The MC stopped
halfway up the stairs and shrugged.

"Drum solo!"

One yell was all it took: the crowd found its voice and the bar got noisy again. Hank looked back at the MC, who said, "You've got time for one more."

Hank sat back on the throne and picked the sticks up off the snare. The crowd cheered. He pushed the kick pedal a couple of times, the hammer thudding against the head, sending low end out into the crowd and quieting them down. He looked down at his hands, at the sticks. He set them back on the snare and stood up from the kit.

"You guys mind if I play a song with chords?"

The bar erupted in unison, a chorus of disappointed *aaah*. "No drum solo man?"

"No drum solo." He walked around to the front of the stage. "And no more drinks for the asshole who keeps shouting drum solo." The crowd laughed. Hank looked around the stage for Dizzy's guitar, but couldn't find it. "Anybody have an acoustic?" He put his hand over his eyes, a visor from the lights. An acoustic guitar floated across the top of the crowd and landed in his hands. He pulled the strap over his head. "Now you've got to be really quiet"—he pointed at Dizzy's amp—"because I'm sure as hell not plugging into that." He stepped out in front of the microphone, to the front of the stage, just past the flood of lights. "And you'll have to forgive me. I only know four chords." He picked out the four he knew and sang:

I knew a man spent all his life
Selling insurance in case of fire
Or some act of God come crashing down
Burning all his things into the ground
But when Death came through
He did not care
No insurance
Could save him from those stairs

Your bones get old before you know

That man's wife she asked me how
Was she supposed to know what to do now
I could not say, I had not thought
Of what the living do
When the dead is all they got
But I'd tell her now: do what you want
I know ghosts don't choose
Where they get to haunt

And your bones get old before you know

I spend my days picking up the dead
Most of them dying in their beds
But no not me, I will not go
Lying on my back waiting for Death to show
I'll stretch my legs and split this town
And Death can do his best to track me down

Your bones get old before you know

∞

"Mrs. Galloway?" The old woman peered out between the door and the threshold.

"Hello," she said. Like a question again, but this time with good reason.

"It's Hank. From the funeral home?" Now his voice was doing it too, turning up the end of the phrase.

"Can I help you? Is there a problem?" She sounded scared. Or sad. Her voice shook and Hank couldn't tell which it was. Maybe just old age.

"No problem, ma'am. I just have something to tell you is all." Hank looked at his boots and kicked a stray rock back into the planter on the side of the cement steps. "Do you mind if I step inside?"

"I'd rather you not." Her voice was still shaky and he knew it was fear. He took a step back and imagined what it must look like from her perspective: a punk kid in his boots and jeans showing up on her porch after dark. He hadn't meant to come so late. He hadn't been able to decide whether to come at all and then, when he finally did decide, it was late, or at least late for an old woman, but he didn't want to sleep on it because he knew he would change his mind.

Sometimes the rash thing is the right thing.

"I understand." He didn't quite know how to start, talking to a stranger through a crack in the door. "I have two things to tell you, but I only really want to say the one. Just now, I told you there were two things because I knew if I said that, then I would be committing to saying both of them—the one that I want to say and the one that I don't want to say." He stopped, hoping she might stop him, slam the door like he was selling vacuums or something. But Teddy sold insurance; she wasn't slamming the door. "The first then—the one I want to tell you—is this: You've got a lot to live for. I mean, just having breath, that's something, right? You're probably thinking, 'Some nerve, this kid' and you're probably right. In fact, I can't even tell you why I'm here—this isn't something I usually do. But when you asked before, 'What do I do now,' I knew you weren't talking about who you call or whatever. I knew you meant, 'What do I do now,' like now that Teddy's gone." Hank's voice went weak at the man's name. "I mean your husband, now that your husband is gone."

"You remembered his name."

"I guess I did." He remembered the whole scene, minute by minute, he couldn't stop running it. He couldn't tell from her voice, but he pictured her smiling a little, behind the door. Then he pictured her crying, at the sound of the name, and he didn't want to picture anything anymore. So he spoke: "I don't know exactly what you do now. I'm no expert. I'm just a kid, really. But I've been thinking about what I do, what any of us do, just zombie-walking through, you know, trying to get from point A to point B and I guess we should have a better idea of how easy it is to die—I should have a better idea anyway, what with picking up bodies all day. And you should too, now. So I think maybe we should do what we want. I mean, I don't know exactly what that is and I didn't know your husband—"

"Teddy."

"Right. I didn't know Teddy. But it seems to me that he'd want you to do what you want to do. Does that make sense?" Hank let the question hang in the quiet for a minute before he realized it was rhetorical.

"And the second thing?" she asked.

"The second thing. And I don't really know why I need to tell you this, because I didn't do anything wrong, not here anyway, not at your house. But maybe the action itself is wrong. Maybe the motivation, the intention is wrong."

"Get to it, son."

Hank took a deep breath, filling his cheeks, before letting most of it out through his nose. The last of the air escaped through his lips in a quiet pop. "I checked your husband's pockets for money. I don't know why I did it—I don't know why I do it. I just—I'm sorry is all. I didn't take anything. He didn't have anything to take. But I don't want to make excuses, I just want to say I'm sorry and it was dumb and wrong and rotten and I'm sorry."

There was a long pause and Hank thought he might just say goodbye and walk back down the steps. Or maybe just nod and leave. Then he heard it: her tiny, shaky soprano, squeaking and sputtering, a gentle version of Dizzy's amp, a high-pitched squeal rolling into a squawk. "Are you laughing, Mrs. Galloway?" And she was. He could hear her behind the door, trying in vain to stifle the sound.

"I'm sorry—I'm—I'm sorry. I shouldn't laugh. It's not funny, is it?" She swung the door open and Hank saw the tears on her face.

"I didn't mean to—shit. Sorry! Shoot. Did I make you—are you crying because—"

She wiped her face with the back of her hand. "Son, I'm crying for all sorts of reasons. I miss my Teddy. I don't know what to do. And here you are offering some kind of confession—acting the priest and telling me to do what I need to do and then coming clean to relieve yourself of the burden—and to think, no money! Teddy always—*always*—kept cash on him. He was terrified of getting somewhere and not having money with him. He was obsessive about it. Constantly checking his pockets to make sure his wallet was still there. Walked around patting himself on the rear, like a crazy person. I would do the laundry and would have to check every pocket of every pant and shirt. And he stiffed you. Stiffed!" She had been keeping her laughter in check, but at *stiffed* she lost it altogether, snorting, gasping to catch her breath. Hank watched as her face shifted, sounds of laughter mixing with sobs, tears welling and then running down her cheeks. She brought her hands to her face and her tiny shoulders began to shake. Hank was glued to the steps, his hands in his pockets, unsure of what should happen next. He didn't have to decide; Mrs. Galloway lurched forward, across the threshold and his hands shot from his pockets, his arms wrapping her thin frame, her face pressed into his chest.

"You smell like cigarettes," she said.

Hank raised his eyebrows. "I'm sorry?"

"It's nice, really." She pulled away to look at him, but kept her arms around him. Hank thought for a second about Dizzy, about what he would say if he saw the two of them. "Teddy quit smoking ten years ago." She smiled. "Better policy." She pressed her face back into his jacket and inhaled, deep and loud.

"You want one?" he asked, reaching for the pack in his pocket.

"A cigarette?" She looked at him, feigning shock. "At my age?" Hank pulled out the box, wrapped in a rubber band, holding a pack of matches. He slid two cigarettes from the package and put one of them in his mouth. He struck a match, lit the cigarette, and whipped the flame out. She watched the whole process, a funny look on her face, her eyes and mouth caught between smiling and remembering and wondering. He held the second cigarette up and shrugged his shoulders.

"I should do what I want, right?" she said. And she pinched her fingers together and pulled the cigarette out of his mouth, filled her lungs, and watched him strike another match.

The Favorite Season

The Favorite Season

Ain't it the truth that we've trad-ed our youth for gray hair and wrink-led skin.

Ain't it a lie that when good things do die they ne-ver do live a-gain. Woah-

Ooh_____ Ooh_____

oh_____ Woah-oh___ Woah-oh_____ Woah-oh___ Woah-

Woah_____

oh_____

The Smell of Burning Leaves

"I play party music. I turn my amp up, bring my arm down, and holler." When he said it, he looked away from her, turning to the green grass beneath the old bench.

She wasn't fooled. "You ever listen to Miles Davis?"

He shook his head.

"When you talk, I think of his trumpet. You should sing that way," she said.

"A trumpet?" he asked. "Is that supposed to be a compliment?"

∞

"Fall's my favorite season." When she said it, he knew he would sing it. His mind was already humming.

"It smells like death, but I like all the colors. And the smell, actually," she said.

He hushed the humming in his head. "The smell of death?" He was curious and he wanted her to keep talking. He liked her quiet voice, it felt like she was always telling secrets.

"You know. The smell of burning leaves. Didn't they do that where you grew up? We had one weekend in the fall where everyone would rake their leaves into piles and burn them. It was kinda weird—the fire department was on high alert, standing at attention, and families were burning leaves in the yard. My sisters and I would beg my dad not to burn them, so we could keep jumping in them. All the red and orange and yellow. They looked like fire, and then they were fire."

"The smell of fall and the smell of death. I guess I never thought of it like that."

"No you didn't, did you?" It was an observation, not an inquisition. "You probably never noticed. There's a difference."

"I've seen leaves change," he insisted.

"Have you though? Have you *seen* leaves change? Watched them?"

"I've seen the colors. I go with a couple guys to the Boundary Waters every fall." He stretched his arms above his head, recalling the weight of the aluminum canoe on his shoulders. "It's my favorite place."

"But you've never watched the colors *change*."

"Waited and watched?" he asked. "Like paint drying?"

"No. Just noticed. Appreciated. Reveled."

"Revelry is for the summer."

"Like party music right?" She laughed, like her voice, like a secret. "Why are the Boundary Waters your favorite place?"

He looked her in the eyes, cocking his head a little, wondering what all was in there. "I like the quiet."

"The quiet? What about your hollering?"

He smiled, lips together. "I was gonna go once by myself, after college. All alone for a couple of weeks. I drew up the plans, just to go—I don't know—find myself? I thought if I could just get silence for long enough—" He trailed off. "Anyway. I never went."

"Why?"

"Other things, I guess."

"I like your big ideas," she said.

"You better." He reached across the porch, to where she was sitting, cross-legged, in the fold out chair. He touched her cheek. "Because you're gonna have to put up with my follow-through."

∞

"Things end you know," she said. "One of us will die first."

The leaves had lost their color. In the last moments of fall, before the cold came in, they sat on the porch, her crying, him looking at his hands, not knowing what to do with them. He had just returned from the woods. There was always something to do with your hands in the woods.

"I don't understand," he whispered. "I left for four days. What did I miss?" She nuzzled her head into his shoulder, into his chest. He got his fingers stuck trying to run them through her hair.

"Ouch. Hey—just—"She grabbed his hand and pulled it out of the mess, laughing, her face still wet.

"It's different than splitting wood." He was sheepish about it, a new feeling around her.

"You didn't miss anything. It's not your fault. It's not you."

"Wow." He stood up and wove his fingers together, pulling and cracking his knuckles. "That's the worst line ever."

"It's the end of October," she said.

"Yes it is," he said. She looked up at him. The crying started in her eyes, not in the mouth like most people. He watched it happen, noticed it, like changing leaves. "Is it cheesy to say it's not the end of us though?"

"Yes it is," she snorted. "Super cheesy." She wiped her nose on the sleeve of her red sweatshirt. "But I don't mind."

∞

"What do you do in the winter then? It's not the season for party time music."

"Party time music? No. Party music. Party time music makes it sounds like I play for preschoolers."

"Whatever. Party music then. What do you do in the winter?"

"I still play party music. That way everyone can have a party time. Party time!" He pumped a fist. "Maybe I'll change it. Maybe we'll start calling it party time music."

She watched his eyes go, the rest of his insides leaving the room with them. She was never sure where he went, but she didn't care as long as he came back.

"I should make T-shirts," he mused.

"Maybe you could spend all winter making T-shirts."

"Not a bad idea." He stood up and she saw that she had lost him for the time. She knew about losing things. She walked to the kitchen and poured a cup of coffee, holding the sugar dispenser above the cup for a long time, adding half-and-half from the refrigerator. She liked the swirl of black to cream when she dipped her spoon in the mug.

"How can you stand it with all the sugar?"

She handed the mug to him. "Try it." He took it from her and sipped from the rim of the glass.

"It's so sweet."

"You only live once. And it's winter outside. I deserve some sweetness."

"You're like a T-shirt machine today. *I Deserve Some Sweetness*. That's even better than *Party Time Music*."

She took the mug back from him. "Glad I could help."

∞

"I've been thinking about what you said."

"About what?" she asked.

"About how one of us will die first." He looked at the ground and she was nervous that it was more than just his eyes that would leave her. "And the end of October. I mean now that I know about your mom and your sister and all that. I guess—I mean it must be hard."

She looked at him and clenched her molars, waiting for what she knew was coming. "Yes?"

"And I know I'm a bit of a mess. Like sometimes it must feel like I'm eleven different people or something. Sometimes it feels like that in my head anyway, so I can't imagine what that must be like for you." He looked at her across the porch. It was the first warm day in ages. The air was wet and the snow was falling off the trees in clumps. She kept him there, with her eyes, kept him in the moment.

"It's not so bad," she breathed.

"But maybe it is. Maybe you just don't want to say." He squinted his eyes, like he was looking for something. "But I have something to say. I want you to think about all this—really think about it— before you say something back. I want you to know that I never feel more like myself than when I'm with you. All winter here, hibernating, I've never felt more comfortable in my skin."

In the woods behind the apartment, a branch broke, under the weight of the snow. They both turned their heads in the direction of the sound. She was the first to come back. He stayed in the woods.

"People do what they're gonna do, you know?" he continued. "And I guess I'm used to that, doing what I want to do and not worrying about it. But now I'm worrying about it." He turned back to her. "I'm not supposed to worry about anything, you know?" He laughed. "I play party time music, right?" He saw that she didn't know what she was supposed to say. "But now I worry about you."

"Why?"

"No, no," he shook his head, "I've said it wrong. Don't misunderstand me. What I mean is: I like worrying about you. And I like you worrying about me."

"And?"

"And so I'm changing my vote. Or changing my mind maybe."

"About me?"

"About summer being my favorite," he said. "I'll take spring. Give me leaves turning green and birds coming home." He scuffed the grass under the bench, kicking away the snow to see the advent of green. "One of us will die first. But until then I'd like to stay here."

My Father's Favorite Hymn

Luke Hawley

Paul Dudrey

Moderato

1. I dug my fa-ther up in Mich-i-gan. If it's a sin,
2. And when they laid him in the ground Six hun-dred miles down
3. I took my son to see his grave Out by Well Lake,

I would do it a-gain. I drove his bo-dy o-ver four state lines.
from my home town, I shook my fist and cursed the Lord of Hosts,
off the in-ter-state. And though my faith is grow-ing dim.

If it's a crime, I would do it a thou-sand times.
the one he loved the most, And swore to do right by his ghost.
I taught him then my fa-ther's fav'-rite hymn.

It is well with my soul Now he's bur-ied in the Min-ne-so-ta
It is well with my soul Though my spi-rit's wan-der's deep in-to the

snow. It is well with my soul.
cold. It is well with my soul.

In the mad-ness of this

My Father's Favorite Hymn

Halfway Home

I

On potluck Sundays in the winter, after
Gregory's dad delivered the sermon, he and his
brothers joined the congregation in the kitchen
downstairs and prayed over the folding tables
bending under the weight of food, and ate all the
hotdish they could stomach, before racing outside to
the empty field across the street. The field had been
flooded, like every open field in the city, to give
people a place to skate. They pulled skates off the
hooked end of their sticks, slipped them on their
feet and, starting with the laces closest to their toes,
pulled them taut, one by one, up the length of the
boot.

Someone would unpocket a puck and they
would flip it in the snow to decide who would pick
first. Because there were three of them, Gregory and
his brothers were never the captains and, even
though he was the youngest, he was always picked
first. He would face off against one of his brothers,
running his right hand down the wood handle, his
knuckles almost scraping the ice, the curve of his
stick slapping and calling for the game to start. The
puck would drop and he would be home, the wind
in his face, the ice under his feet, striding the length
of the frozen field. His father would appear on the
edge of the ice, rubbing his hands together for
warmth, smiling, watching his boys battle.

II

He was holding a hose—dousing the fire that was burning a house to the ground—when a face in the flames told him that his father was dead. It wasn't a real person's face, not a human face, just as the smoldering house wasn't a real job. The old place had been donated to the academy and the ghost in the fire just sort of floated up in the flames to tell Gregory that his father was dead. He dropped the hose he was holding and let the water spray where it wanted.

Gregory never believed in much—not ghosts anyway—but for whatever reason he knew it was true, then and there, what the face said to him, that his father was dead. He got the call that night from his older brother about the accident. And when his brother mentioned the burns, Gregory was not surprised.

That night he dreamt he was standing at the bottom of a hill. His dad throttles by him, motorcycle all black and chrome, leaning hard around the corner. He shouts for him to slow down, to stop showing off, to watch out for the crest of the hill, but the bike's engine is too loud, his father guns it to climb the hill and his voice is drowned out. Gregory watches him rise up the road and float over the summit of the hill. For a moment he sees nothing—his father is lost over the horizon. Gregory is sure he is only driving away, he will turn the bike around and come back, cackling like he has just told one of his terrible jokes. Gregory waits to hear the slow rumbling of the engine as his father turns the bike around but it never comes.

They buried him in Michigan, where his parents had moved two years before. Gregory made the trip from Minnesota and met his brothers at a strange church and the three of them wrapped their arms around their mother. Gregory saw the closed casket over her shoulder. It looked like maple, stained to a deep brown. Nothing about the scene seemed right, nothing felt natural. The church wasn't right, the pews were filled with strangers, and he had never heard his father's voice projecting from the stage where his body lay.

After the funeral he had gone back to Minnesota and quit the fire academy. He'd been head of his class and the academy called him to come back, but how could he explain the ghost in the fire? He was done believing in things that weren't there. That was the business of his father and what good had it done him? He would look for a job laying brick or mudding sheetrock, something he could wrap his hands around, something that would leave a residue he could wash clean. He bought a pickup truck and a ring and he and his girlfriend got married at the courthouse because he was never going to set foot inside a church again.

They spent a lot of time at the lake house his wife's family owned. His father-in-law took him hunting and fishing. Taught him how to field dress a deer. Where to catch walleye. And at the end of the day Gregory washed the blood from his hands using anything he could find—clear water, hard dirt, white snow. He immersed himself in ten thousand lakes and buried his heart in the North Woods.

He came home from work one Wednesday to find his wife smiling, buzzing in her skin. "I'm pregnant," she said. She said everything would be new and better now, everything would change. Nothing really did though, except the shape of her stomach. He kept the winter in his heart and she grew a baby boy in the warmth of her stomach.

III

"The only thing I really like about Catholicism is sainthood," his wife said.

Gregory's father had preached at a non-denominational community church but his wife's family was Catholic. It was a point of contention between Gregory and the rest of his family. He had explained that she was more of a lapsed Catholic. He should have explained that he wasn't much of anything anyway.

"In my book, your dad was a Saint," she continued.

It was winter and they were at the cabin. He knew she wanted him to talk about what he was feeling, but he didn't have anything to say. He kept it for himself. He was content to let her do all the talking.

"There should be a special gravesite for him, where people could gather and lay flowers," she said. "Like for a Venerable. He deserves that."

She arched her back across the arm of the couch and rubbed her pregnant belly. He wanted to curl up in there and wrap his arms tight around his son and hibernate like bears.

He spent the next day clearing brush. A straightline had come through late in the summer and dismembered several old trees. Best practice was to clear the branches out after the leaves had fallen. It made the job of dragging them out of the woods easier. He spent all day piling branches on the ice in the middle of the lake, sweating through his long underwear, watching his hot breath turn to steam in the cold air. After dinner, after his wife had gone to bed, he grabbed a can of diesel from the shed and walked out onto the lake. The wind was blowing and he cursed winter under his breath. He should have burned the branches earlier when he was warm from the work. He poured the diesel over the branches and dropped a match on the heap of sticks and brambles. The diesel caught immediately and it was only a moment before the entire pile was lit. He took his gloves off and warmed his hands by the fire, watching the smoke billow into the cold, clear night.

He thought about his wife, asleep, lying on her
side with her hand over her expanding belly,
sprawled out across the length of the bed. He
thought about his mother, lying alone, keeping to
her side of the mattress. He thought about his father.
The Saint. He was beginning to forget the shape of
his father's face. He was beginning to forget the
sound of his voice. Sometimes he could hear it, but
now only in the lilting tone of a minister, not in the
way he actually spoke, but in the way he preached
on Sundays. Gregory sang softly to himself: *The
trump shall resound and the Lord shall descend,
even so, it is well with my soul.* His father's favorite
hymn. His father's voice coming from his lungs.

He looked down at his feet. His toes were
going numb. The fire was safe to burn the rest of the
way down. He turned to head back to the cabin,
looking one more time into the hot coals of the fire.

IV

He was glad he fixed the wipers before he left.
His wife had reminded him about the wipers. She
wasn't exactly on board with the trip. Thirty-four
weeks in and she didn't like him going to the store,
let alone across four states. She was concerned
about the legal ramification. He promised he'd do it
in a day and drive the speed limit there and back.
He had changed the wipers and checked the lights
and the tags. He assured her that she had nothing to
worry about. He explained it had to be done before
his son was born and he stuck out his father's

stubborn chin, so she reminded him about the wipers. He took it as her blessing.

Gregory reached across his body for the Styrofoam cup perched on the dash. It felt good to stretch his arms. He sipped the coffee, now lukewarm, keeping his right hand on the lower part of the steering wheel. Blue-gray clouds rolled over the truck. Gregory checked the rearview mirror. The corners of the black tarp stretched across the bed of the truck flitted in the wind. He had taken the ferry from Milwaukee to Muskegon and now drove Interstate 96 in the dark of night. On the way home, in the light of morning, he would stick to Interstate 90, through Chicago, through Milwaukee, and on across Wisconsin.

He passed a sign for Lansing and the clouds shifted to deep silver. A misty precipitation crystallized on the windshield and Gregory flipped the switch for the wipers.

Gregory walked around the side of the truck and pulled a long piece of PVC from the bed. He set one end of the pipe on the roof of the cab and balanced the other on the canoe rack at the far end of the bed. He steadied the pipe with his hand and walked back to the front of the truck. Pulling the winch wire from under the front bumper, he looped it through the end of the pipe. He hoped it would keep the wire from scratching the paint. He fed the wire through the pipe until he heard the hooked-end clang against the tailgate.

To his left, a rabbit darted under a streetlight. Gregory looked east to where the sun would appear over the horizon in a few hours.

His shoulders were level with the top of the hole. He could make out the shadow of his pickup, parked along the gravel road, ten or twelve yards off to his right. He was thankful for a near full moon— no need for headlights. And he was thankful for no security. No graveyard shift.

Gregory struck the dirt at his feet with the blade of the shovel and brought the handle to his waist, balancing the shovelful with the force of his left arm, his right hand the pivot. He threw the dirt up onto the mound next to the hole and swung the shovel back into the ground. The tip stopped halfway into its swing, a hollow thud sounded underneath what was now a thin layer of dirt and clay. He knelt down and brushed the dirt away. Smooth maple boards. He swept the dirt around the edges of the hole uncovering a dull, silver handle. He stood and slid the shovel along the fine finish of the casket, careful not to scratch the wood. *One shovelful, two shovelfuls, three shovelfuls.* Kneeling again, he ran his rough, red palms along the wood and found the handle on the opposite side of the box.

Gregory tossed the shovel out of the hole and pulled himself up onto the grass. He lay back for moment, stretching his shoulders and back. He could feel his muscles tighten; he would be sore in the morning. The moon was bright enough to wash out most of the stars. He looked to the west for Orion, but it was too early, the hunter didn't show his face until after deer season. Gregory rolled onto his side and lifted himself off the ground. He walked to the truck and opened the door, scanning the cemetery. He popped the shifter into neutral and turned the key in the ignition so the wheel wouldn't lock. He pushed the truck forward with his shoulder and steered with his right hand. He was glad the ground was flat and the plots next to his father's were empty.

He dropped the tailgate and pulled a pair of tow straps from the bed. He lowered himself into the hole and steadied himself on top of the casket. He bent down and, on each side of the casket, hooked a tow strap to the middle handle, where he and one of his brothers had been stationed. He stood up and grabbed the hook at the end of the winch wire, where he attached the tow straps. He pulled himself out of the hole and walked back to the front of the truck. He punched the button marked *UP* and winced, shushing the squeak and strain of the wire pulling his father from the ground.

V

Halfway home in the middle of the afternoon, the sky darkened. Gregory, remembering his promise to his wife, turned the lights on. He had seen a dozen or so police officers and every time he passed one his chest tightened. He scripted the scene in his head:

"Hello Officer."

"What you got in the back?"

"My father."

"Your father?"

"My dead father."

"Your dead father?"

"Yes, Officer. There is precedent for this sort of thing."

Gregory pulled on the wheel of the truck, taking a slight right off the interstate. From the radio, Hank Williams sang *Cold, Cold Heart,* his deep voice sounding funny and thin through the old truck's small speakers. He rolled the wheel around, hand over hand, just like his dad had taught him, and turned left onto the small highway that ran back over the interstate, heading north.

Two miles down the highway, Gregory turned right again, onto a gravel road. It was dark and he blinked his eyes to focus them. He leaned forward in the seat, pulling his chest to the wheel, almost laying his chin on it. He had been traveling for thirty-one hours.

He passed a green sign on his left that read:
Well Lake, ¼ Mile. He had found it on a map last
week. Sixteen miles from his house and he had
never heard of it, never once been there to fish. He
pulled off the gravel onto a snowmobile trail and
stopped a hundred feet in, where the trees grew too
close together to drive any farther. He could see the
lake through the trees that grew along the shore. It
was a small lake, reedy and overgrown with algae in
parts. It was perfect.

He forced open the truck door, knocking his
knee into the metal of the frame. He stepped down
onto the grass and was glad to feel the loamy
softness of the soil under his feet. It would make the
job much easier. In Michigan, it had been hard dirt,
packed by a backhoe, a thick beard of sod growing
over the top of it.

Gregory walked to the rear of the truck,
unbinding bungee cords as he went, pulling on the
tarp, still wet from rain he passed through near Eau
Claire. He reached under the tarp and found the
wooden-handled spade. He hung the metal end over
his shoulder and walked around to the front of the
truck where the headlights shined on a flat patch of
grass. Placing the bridge of his booted foot on the
right side of the metal scoop, he pushed the spade
into the ground. He hopped off of his other foot and
buried the shovelhead, pulling back on the handle
with his two hands. The skin of his hands was
cracked and the pressure on his palms burned. He

moved his right hand down the length of the handle
and lifted the first ladle of dirt.

VI

There was another dream. It is Sunday
afternoon and he is on the ice, his skates underneath
him, stick in hand. He looks down at the blades of
his skates, at the center ice where the puck will
drop. He runs his hands down the shaft of the stick,
readying himself for action, feeling the smooth
wood grain against his palms. Always a wood stick.
It was the way hockey was supposed to be played,
crooked sticks and round rocks. He waits for the
puck, seeing his breath in front of his face,
clenching and unclenching his grip on the stick. It
must be one of his brothers across from him; they
are older, slower, and he will win the faceoff, he
will not break his concentration. He can feel the
blood running through his hands, through the
chambers of his heart, to his freezing feet, wrapped
tight in his skates, to the vein in his forehead. He
waits and waits, but nothing drops, and when he
can't wait any longer, he breaks his focus and looks
up.

The ice is empty. He can see the church across
the street. His father is on the steps, calling him.
"Boy!" he says. "We're leaving now!" Gregory
begins to skate, starting slowly, but picking up
speed. He swings his arms, he pumps his legs. He
drops his stick. He shakes his hands out of his mitts.
"Boy!" his father yells again, "Don't think I won't

leave you!" He tries to call out for him, to ask him to wait, to tell his father he is coming as fast as he can, but he can't find the breath. He looks down at the ice, focusing his energy on his form, on his speed. But the blades of his skates are cutting too deep into the ice. He can see the water underneath. His father is beckoning him, waving his arm. The ice cracks and groans on all sides. He pushes harder, his legs propel him forward. The ice has disappeared, he is gliding on water. He looks down at his skates, at the water. He is sinking. He calls out for his father, but he is no longer there.

Electric Blues

Luke Hawley

Joe Mann

Electric Blues

me-mo - ry
a - ny - thing

With - out you

And your e - lec - tric blues Tel - ling

me (Tel - ling me) it' - ll be (it' - ll be) al -

right

right

Snow Angels

Ethyl turned the wheel hand over hand, like Ronald had taught her when they were teenagers. The Buick drifted down a long driveway flanked on each side by snow, piled high against an old ranch fence. A canary-yellow two-story came into view.

It was her daughter's idea, a visit with Lillian Grey, the mother of a friend. She had been through it, her daughter said, might do some good to talk about it all. Ethyl did not consider herself a person in need of pity, but if it would stop her daughter's phone calls, then she would go.

Ethyl surveyed the wooded acreage on her way up to the stoop. She stomped her boots on the welcome mat and knocked on the front door. The woman who answered the door was tall and fit. Ethyl couldn't believe Lillian had children in their late forties. Her hair was a mess of white and gray tumbling down her back and when Lillian led her into the living room, Ethyl thought of willow trees and the smell of summer.

"Take your shoes off, dear, make yourself comfortable," chirped Lillian, flashing a mouthful of veneers.

Ethyl reached her hand up and patted her tight, white perm. The house felt open to Ethyl, a house she could breathe in. The furniture was sparse and the hardwood floors were stained a golden brown. It was quiet. Simple and elegant, something out of *Good Housekeeping*, Ethyl thought. She slipped off her boots and sat down on a red leather loveseat.

Lillian bunched her oversized sweater at her elbows. "Whiskey or wine?"

"Oh," Ethyl stuttered, "I don't really drink."

"You don't *really* drink or you don't drink?"

"I guess I don't drink. Or I haven't in a long time anyway."

Lillian took a step back, like she was leveling a painting. Her staring made Ethyl uncomfortable. Then: "Whiskey, I do believe."

Ethyl's mouth pinched into a tight smile. "You have a beautiful house, Lillian," Ethyl echoed off the hardwood, as she watched her circumvent a long dining room table to get to a hutch in the corner.

"Please. It's Lily. And thank you." Lily set the bottle and two small tumblers on the coffee table next to a bowl of mixed nuts. She unscrewed the lid and filled each glass almost to the rim. She handed one glass to Ethyl and sat across from her on a matching brown leather couch. Ethyl hesitated.

"I just—I'm not sure—"

Lily interrupted, "You hardly know me right? I understand." She had a ferocity that made Ethyl fidget. "I'm Lily Grey, originally from Houston, Texas. I'm a Leo. I love the summer but I've come to appreciate the cold. That about does it. You?"

Ethyl realized that she wanted to impress Lily more than she had anyone since meeting Ronald. She took a deep breath. "I'm Ethyl." She stopped. "I've always been from here. And I'm a Virgo but I have no idea what that means."

Lily nodded. "Of course. A Virgo. Well, Ethyl-the-Virgo-who's-always-been-from-here I've found it best at times like this to skip formalities and just drink. But if you prefer a toast—" Lily lifted her glass and cocked her head, "—here's to being old enough to know better and too old to care."

Ethyl lifted the glass and sipped. It burned and she covered her mouth with her fist to cough. She set the glass back in her lap. The liquid radiated out to the tips of her body. She wondered if Ronald was due for his pain medication.

Lily read her mind. "My daughter tells me—through your daughter of course—that your husband had a couple toes amputated yesterday."

Ethyl sipped from the glass. She didn't care for the taste, but she liked the fizzle and the warmth. "Three, actually. He wanted to shovel the driveway. I just fell asleep. I was so tired. I reminded him about the hat and gloves but not the socks." She paused. "I don't know how I ever kept up with three kids."

"You were fifty years younger, dear." Lily motioned at her with the glass in her hand. "No sipping in my house, dear. To sweethearts and wives. Skål."

Ethyl nodded. What a strange woman, she thought. Vivacious almost to aggression. She liked her though. The alcohol made her nervous, but on the other hand, she didn't want to seem like a prude. She wondered what Ronald would think. Would he care? Did he even think of her? She sipped again, setting the rim of the glass against her teeth for a moment before speaking. "But he's only one man. And he doesn't move as fast as the kids did. He told me he just got tired and laid down." She shook her head. "Not even a child would do that."

"It's a great mystery, what happens to the mind." Lily said, finishing her glass and setting it down on the table. She filled it up again and reached the bottle across the table and topped off Ethyl's.

Ethyl looked at the glass and put a hand on her perm. She glanced around the house, to the stairway, back to the kitchen. All the lights were off. "Where is your husband?"

"He's at a home." Lily swirled the whiskey and Ethyl wondered if that was why the glasses were called tumblers. "It's why I can keep whiskey in the house. He used to get a glass and fill it and fill it and fill it again. I thought he was just a drunk." Lily stopped. "But he couldn't remember. How was I supposed to know?" And she laughed.

"The doctor wants me to put Ronald in a home." Ethyl watched as Lily gulped another mouthful down, wiping excess whiskey with her sleeve. It seemed an unrefined and unnatural movement for her.

"Will you?" Lily asked.

"I don't know." Ethyl pursed her lips. She avoided thinking about it. "I don't want to." What if he's happier there? "But what if he's better off?"

"That's the question." Lily leaned back into the couch and stretched her arms.

"I can't stand the thought of it." Ethyl picked up her glass. "I'd have to sell the house. Move into an apartment. Where would my kids stay when they came to see us? A hotel? I spent my whole life under that roof with that man." She found her whole body was shaking, her hands tight around the tumbler. She brought the glass to her lips and in two quick gulps, finished the whole of it. "Can you point me to your powder room, please, Lilly?"

"Down the hall, first door on the left." She said, grabbing a handful of nuts. "Cashews are great for your cholesterol," she nodded to the nuts, as she picked through the mix.

Ethyl balanced her way down the hall to the bathroom. Her face flushed with the alcohol. It had been a long a time since dinner. She opened the bathroom door and found the light switch on the wall inside. She stood at the mirror, holding on to both sides of the sink. Her skin hung loose on her face, wrinkled and pale. She looked a million years old, older than dirt, older than flesh allowed.

She turned her veiny hands over and over and tried to remember being young. When they first got married, Ronald rode a motorcycle, wore tight jeans and white t-shirts. His blue eyes buzzed and his laugh bellowed and her love for him was big as the winter sky. Before the kids were born, they had ridden that motorcycle down through the Superior National Forest to Chicago, where they caught old Route 66 and took it all the way to California.

She ran the water and splashed some up on her face. She pulled a hand towel from the rack and dried her face. She tried to smooth the hair on the top of her head but it was frizzing and she didn't have a comb. Through an octagonal window, she spied a small building, a shed or something, twenty feet or so feet from the backdoor. She thought how nice it must be to have space, to live just outside of town.

She walked back down the hallway, where Lily sat at the couch. There were two king-sized slices of chocolate cake laid out on the table, on either side of the whiskey bottle. Her glass had been refilled.

"Cake?" Lily asked. "It's not as good for the cholesterol. But it tastes better than nuts."

Ethyl was out of points. She didn't know how much whiskey counted for, but she knew she didn't have room for the cake. "I don't know."

"If it sways you, I have ice cream in the freezer."

Ethyl took great pride in never swaying, in always counting her Weight Watcher points and giving everything its fair value. She had built a life on principle. But principle tasted like mixed nuts and rice cakes and she deserved a break.

"Ice cream?" She blew a sigh out of puffed-up cheeks. "Of course then. I'd love some." Lily took the cake back into the kitchen. Ethyl picked up her glass and helped herself to another full swallow. She cleared her throat and set the glass back down.

Lily came back into the living room. She handed the cake to Ethyl.

"I really shouldn't eat this whole thing." Ethyl insisted.

Lily dug her fork into the cake and cut out a piece the size of her mouth. "Shouldn't?"

"Thirty-two years of Weight Watchers and I've never paid a cent. Until yesterday." Ethyl shook her head. "I missed my weigh-in. And you know what? I was angry at Ronald. The doctors took three of his frozen toes and I was mad about missing my weigh-in. It's terrible. I just get so angry sometimes."

"You've got to let go, honey." Lily forked at the cake on Ethyl's plate. "Screw Weight Watchers."

Ethyl scooped a piece of cake and a heap of vanilla ice cream onto her fork and into her mouth. She chewed and moaned: "Oh my God. It's delicious."

"An old family recipe. Stolen by Betty Crocker and put in a box." Lily winked.

Ethyl couldn't finger the culprit, the whiskey or the sugar, but she could feel her muscles slack. "I feel like all the things I've devoted my life to are disappearing. Ronald, Weight Watchers. My kids live hundreds of miles from here. You know what I mean?" She looked up at Lily, whose cheeks were full, a crumb of cake on the corner of her mouth. Ethyl laughed and pointed her fork at the corner of Lily's mouth.

Lily smiled, nodding and swallowing. "Sure. But you're still here. You're here talking with me, right? Eating chocolate cake?"

Ethyl tilted her head and looked at Lily. "How do you stay so positive?"

"Liquor?" Lily smirked and set her fork on her empty plate, covering her mouth with the back of her hand. "It's mostly over for me now, you know? I don't live with it anymore. I visit Nathaniel a couple times a week. I find new things to do. I run support meetings. I help out at church. I work out. I make my own schedule." She dropped her hand back into her lap. "I'm only living for one person now. And it's a hell of lot easier."

Ethyl could not imagine. She sat and stared at her for a full minute and couldn't think of one thing to say. She forked the last bit of cake and ice cream into her mouth. She felt guilty about everything. The cake and ice cream. Ronald's toes. She looked at Lily and wondered what it was like to be her, what it was like to have her life. "Don't you feel guilty?" she asked.

Lily looked down at the empty plate she held. "It gets easier. You try to remember that you did what was best for him." When she looked up from the plate, Ethyl saw her small smile on Lily's long face.

"And you throw yourself into other things." She continued, winking again at Ethyl. "Like helping other people. Or like making chocolate cakes and stocking up on ice cream when it's on sale."

Ethyl looked toward the back of the house. "Are you a gardener?"

"Not at all," Lily laughed. "Why do you ask?" Ethyl watched as she raised the whiskey to wash down the last of her cake.

"I just saw the shed out back and figured you must be. Your husband was then?"

"Ah-ha," Lily swallowed. "Not a shed. A sauna."

"A sauna?" Ethyl swallowed the rest of her whiskey. "I've never been in a sauna before."

"You've lived at this latitude your whole life and never been in a sauna?" Lily's eyes widened. "That's insanity. *That's* dementia." Ethyl snorted. Lily set her empty glass down and beckoned for Ethyl's. "One more quick toast and then I'll show you how to enjoy winter, instead of just surviving." She filled the glasses and raised hers. "What do you think Ethyl?"

Ethyl froze. "A toast?"

"A toast."

"Okay then. Well." Ethyl thought about it, but she didn't know any toasts. So she said the first thing that came to her head. "Here's to ten fingers and ten toes?"

Lily roared with laughter. She reached her right hand up to the earring dangling from her lobe. "To ten fingers and ten toes!" She lifted her glass and drained the cup. "Come with me." She stood from the couch and walked back toward the kitchen. Ethyl followed her, steadying herself along the back of the couch. In the kitchen, Lily opened the sliding door and walked out toward the sauna, along a shoveled path. Ethyl stopped at the doorway.

"Don't you want your boots?"

Lily lifted the bottle over her head, beckoning for Ethyl to follow. The stone pathway under her socked feet felt cold. Ethyl giggled and lurched. She opened her eyes wide, stretching her long face, and focused on walking a straight line to the sauna.

"Hurry up!" Lily stood in the doorway, signaling Ethyl to step into the sauna. Inside, the sauna was paneled with cedar planks. Benches ran along the wall on opposite sides of the small room. A bowl of stones sat in the center. "It shouldn't take long to heat up. Nathaniel always built the best for me."

Ethyl inhaled the sweet smell of cedar. "This is amazing."

"We haven't even started yet." Lily slugged from the bottle and handed it to Ethyl. "You're drunk."

"I don't think so." Ethyl looked at the bottle for a moment before tipping it back and taking in a mouthful. She could feel the heat in her cold toes, but she didn't know if it was the alcohol or the sauna.

"If you don't think so, then you are." Lily ladled water from a plastic bucket on the floor and poured it across the rocks. Ethyl listened as the rocks hissed and watched the steam rise. Lily pulled her sweater over her head and set it on the bench next to her. "I sauna every night. Opens your pores and lets the demons out." She tapped a large thermometer on the wall. It was covered in pictures of winter birds. "Already up over seventy. You feeling warm?"

Ethyl ran a hand across her forehead. She was perspiring. "I guess I am. I thought maybe it was the whiskey."

Lily laughed. "Probably a little of both. You'll want to take off your clothes now."

"All my clothes?" Ethyl sat to keep her balance and pulled off her socks.

"That's what I'd suggest." Ethyl looked up from her feet to see Lily's naked body pouring more water on the bowl of rocks.

"Oh my." Ethyl found it hard to look away from Lily. She continued to disrobe, keeping her arms close to her body, ashamed at how her skin hung from her bones. Lily's skin seemed so fair and smooth. Ethyl had never had skin like that.

"No need for modesty in a sauna, Ethyl." Lily lifted her arms across the back of the bench and hung her head back over her shoulders. She shook her head and her hair swung across her breasts.

Ethyl took another drink before removing the last of her clothing. She tried to relax, rolling her head around her neck. She lifted her shoulders and let them drop. Lift and drop, lift and drop.

Lily sighed and pushed her hair back behind her, stretching her shoulders and resting the back of her head in the hammock of her hands. "Ethyl who has-always-been-from-here." She reached across the sauna and took the whiskey from the bench, where it sat next to Ethyl. She eyeballed the contents. "One more good shot apiece, I think." She tipped her head back and took a hungry gulp.

"Nathaniel moved us here when our children were young. I hated him for it. I hated the cold. And the women. I couldn't get any of them to say more than three words to me." She passed the bottle back to Ethyl.

"I don't know. You said it. I'm drunk already."

Lily laughed and Ethyl thought it sounded like a nest of baby birds. "Take it. A gift from me to you."

"Why thank you!" She heard her voice, the drama in it, and she giggled. "I'm sure the women didn't hate you. Not you, Lily!"

Lily smiled back. "Ah, but they did. I was an outsider. I wore too much makeup and, at that time, I drove a convertible."

"I've always wanted a convertible. But it never made good sense with so much winter."

"That was the problem. You women and your good sense. Life's too short for good sense. You should buy one now. They're cheap this time of year. We'll go driving when the sun comes back."

Ethyl thought of her and Lily driving to down to Chicago, rolling the top back, chasing the sun. She felt a new wanting, a leaning towards something.

Lily continued. "It took me a long time, trying to figure out how to assimilate here. And then one winter it hit me. We are the geography that surrounds us. All these women, who seemed so cold and harsh, it was just the icy layer. Snow can be so soft. And warm. And a landscape of snow holds millions of tiny perfect flakes. I just had to adjust my perspective."

Ethyl looked at Lily. Sweat was beading from every pore, running down her skin. She noticed the wrinkles now, the dark spots. Ethyl followed the map of her skin up to her long hair, now wet with perspiration. She made out the faint streaks of coloring. All of the sudden they were the same, two old women, naked, fending off the insurmountable armies of age. "Let's do it. I'll sell the Cadillac and buy a convertible and when it gets warm enough, we'll drive Route 66 out to California." She couldn't believe the words coming from her mouth. The booze had given her the sensation that she was outside her body, watching this strange woman make wild suggestions. Part of her wanted to pour back into her skin, but another part didn't want to take her words back. "What do you say?"

Lily eyes softened. "I love all of you women and your big surprises."

"I don't know what you're talking about," Ethyl stammered.

"You just invited me to California! I never saw that coming from Ethyl-who-has-always-been-from-here."

Ethyl looked down to the cedar board running under their feet. "I guess. But maybe it's not a good idea. Maybe it's the whiskey."

"Are you kidding me? It's a brilliant idea!" She smiled at Ethyl. "You turn to water with a little hot air." Lily stood up. "Alright." She clapped her hands and rubbed them together. "Are you ready?"

"Ready for what?"

"Tradition, Ethyl." Lily offered her hand. "We'll be jumping in the snow."

Ethyl laughed, trying to fill the small sauna. She felt the pull of her old skin. "I don't think so! We could get pneumonia. It could kill us." She put her cautious hand in Lily's.

Lily leaned across the stones, her hair falling all around her face. "Jos ei viina, terva tai sauna auta, tauti on kuolemaksi."

"What's that?" Ethyl asked.

"It's Finish. Nathaniel taught me. If booze, tar, or the sauna won't help, the illness is fatal. No tar, but we've got enough booze and sauna to make up for it. Now drink up. I need you to finish that bottle."

Ethyl stared at Lily, then at the whiskey. She lifted it to her mouth and swallowed, tossed the bottle aside and screamed as the two of them crashed out the door. The snow turned to steam as Ethyl waved her arms and legs, the cold stinging the tips of her nerves, the blood on the brim of her skin.

Savages

Luke Hawley

Joe Mann

1. Don't be a fool   Love is not all just sim‑ple and cool   It's ham‑mer and nails   Ce‑ment and shale   Light‑ning and hail
2. So we pre‑pare   To fight it clean and tough and fair   We put up our fists   Tape up our wrists   And we swing and we hit
3. And we are bound   To fight it toe to toe, round for round   We huff and we puff   We bleed and we scuff   But it's nev‑er e‑nough
4. So we go down   And bust our fa‑ces on the ground   We fight and we fend   Come lose or come win   We fight to the end

Savages

Are we sa - va - ges?

Star - ving and rav - ished Hun - gry to Hun-gry to

be held close be held close And nev-er let go

And nev - er let go

The Clinch

Blakely liked working the door when the temperature dropped below freezing. He sat on his stool, smoking a cigarette, and let his hands go numb. It felt like his fingers were swollen, like the minutes after a fight, before the throbbing and pounding started, when they just felt like fat sausages dangling from his hands.

"Blakely! I need you in here."

Blakely got off his stool and stepped into the bar, eyeballing the crowd for action. The Lucky was dim-lit and dark paneled, making it difficult to see anything. He skimmed the walls, from the Golden Tee machine past the mounted moose head, until he struck on Haunch, owner and tender of The Lucky. Haunch pointed a chubby finger toward the pool table, at a group of good old boys, yelling and laughing.

"The girl," Haunch said.

Blakely headed toward to the corner, past the hightops, past the ladies staring at their straws, past the men staring at the ladies, everybody looking like shadows. Another reason he liked working the door: it was outside. His sponsor said it was a bad idea, employment at The Lucky, but he didn't have a whole lot of options.

"Is there a problem here?"

A red-faced man turned to look at Blakely. "Not yet there isn't."

"Why don't you leave her alone?" suggested Blakely.

"Why don't you leave me alone?" replied the red-faced man.

The girl looked at Blakely. Her eyelids flitted and she stared at the floor. The red-faced man turned his back on Blakely and put his arm around the girl's waist.

"I asked you to leave her alone." Blakely put his hand on the man. The man shrugged it off and turned back around. Blakely smelled the sweetness on his breath and watched his liquor eyes try to focus.

"What are you gonna do about it, old man?"

Blakely filled his lungs and caged the oxygen in the center of his chest. He was old but he would never be used to the name of it. He made one fist, then the other, squeezing his fingers, tightening the skin around his knuckles.

"I'm not going to ask you again," he said.

The man laughed, saliva spraying from his mouth and showering Blakely's face. Then he turned back to the girl and slid his hand further down her back, his fingers slipping into her back pocket. Blakely took another deep breath, charging the blood through his veins and into his fingertips. He put a hand on the man's shoulder. There was no hesitation: the man brought his fist around with the rest of his body and landed a blow across Blakely's face. Blakely unballed his fist and wiggled his fingers. His body bounced a tic, from his feet loosey-goosey up through his shoulders. He looked the man in the eyes, retracted his fingers into a fist, and jabbed him in the face. The man brought his hands to his nose, catching the blood that ran down into his mouth.

"You son of a bitch!" The man swung again, a bear swatting flies, and Blakely shielded his face, catching the blow with his forearm. He swung a quick hook, this time hitting the flesh of the man's cheek. The man clutched his cheek and Blakely jabbed his stomach. He felt his knuckles hit muscle, abs gone flabby on his own frame. The man doubled over, spit turning to vomit, pouring to the floor. "What the hell, man?" It was one of the others, a stretch of arms and legs topped with a camouflage ballcap.

"Get him out of here." Blakely said. "And don't come back." Two of them steadied their friend, arms under his pits, and headed for the door. Blakely looked at the girl. "You alright?"

Her eyes narrowed to slits. "Jesus, man. I can take care of myself." And she followed the men out the door.

∞

"You might as well change your name to Blacky."

Red Eddie called himself a Nazi. Blakely called him an idiot. It wasn't Blakely's idea to let him work out at the gym but he didn't own the gym, so he didn't have any say over who boxed there. His old manager, Frank Rosario, owned the gym, at least he had until his stroke, when he headed to the home and his son-in-law took over the books. The books said anyone who paid could join, and Blakely's job security said he'd train anyone who joined.

"So you won't even fight a black man?" said Blakely. He wasn't black himself, but he knew plenty of fighters that were. The way he figured, people were the same wherever you went, some good, some bad, and it was God's job to sort them out, not his. And certainly not Red Eddie's.

"Hell yeah I'll fight one." Red Eddie bounced from side to side, jabbing his long arms in quick, short strokes, as Blakely held the bag. There wasn't a better feeling for Blakely, holding a bag and taking blows off his whole body, like the moment, in the eighth round or so, when both fighters are exhausted, and they just hang on each other.

"I'll beat the black right off one. Jews too," said Red Eddie. He stopped swinging. "Break their big Jew noses." He laughed a high-pitched squeak.

Blakely didn't laugh. "So what's the difference between me and you?" Blakely asked. He let go of the bag and let it squeak from the low rafters. Everything in the gym made noise—the swinging bag, the groaning mat, the twanging ropes, the rat-a-tat-tat of the speed bag. Lockers ran along the east wall, mirrors along the west and south. It was maybe half the size of a high school gym, without the high roof and the shiny floors. Blakely knew it wasn't much but it didn't matter to him.

Red Eddie stepped back from the bag and dropped his hands at his sides. His tanktop was drenched in sweat, but his hair held tight, perfectly parted and combed over, heavy with pomade. He took his fists from his gloves and reached up to spread the thin Chaplin sprouting below his nose. Blakely thought he looked ridiculous, but he was a good fighter.

"The difference is that I don't talk to them. Unless you count this—" and he jabbed his right fist twice "—as talking." Red Eddie giggled. It echoed off the mirrored walls and wood floors and Blakely balled his fists.

He heard a truck pull into the gravel lot and Blakely looked toward the double doors at the north end of the gym. It was Jennifer, his daughter, off of work, come to get Red Eddie. Blakely thought she looked too skinny, her long hair hanging between her jutting shoulder blades. He wanted to cook her a pre-fight dinner, lots of pasta and bread, maybe some chicken.

"Hey baby!" she yelled across the gym. "Let me see what my man is made of!" Red Eddie roared and grabbed his shirt, ripping it in two, from top to bottom. He hefted a barbell off the floor and chucked it like a hammer toss, over the ring. It skidded across the floor and hit a mirror on the other side of the gym, cracking the glass along the bottom.

"You better hope he's made of money if he keeps that up," Blakely mumbled. "Frank's gonna be pissed."

"Frank's a spic in a wheelchair," Red Eddie snarled. He puts his arms up and flexed his biceps. "He ain't gonna do nothing."

Jennifer hooted. "Baby!" She hung on his arm and kissed his mouth.

Blakely remembered a visit when she was eight. He had taken her to the park down by Deer Creek and she held onto the monkey-bars that same way, while he waited by her side, ready to catch her if she fell. She finished kissing Red Eddie and gave Blakely the same gritty stare she had then, as if to say, *I don't need your help. Ever.*

"Let's get out of here, Eddie. I got an itch I gotta scratch."

Red Eddie grabbed her ass and she screeched and jumped toward the exit.

"See you, old man." Red Eddie smiled, showing all his teeth.

∞

Blakely hated the home, but he went every day to see Frank. It was his way of counting his blessings that all his beatings hadn't caught up with him yet.

"Hey Frank. I brought you some donuts from Mae's." He put the box of a half-dozen old-style glazed on the table next to the bed. He turned to the nurse. "Can we walk?"

She raised an eyebrow. "You can. But Frank here isn't going anywhere." She left the room and returned a minute later with a wheelchair.

The nurse wrapped her arms around Frank's torso to lift him, but Blakely stopped her. "I can do it," he said. She raised the eyebrow again. "I may look worse for wear, but I'm stringy strong," he said.

It was what Frank had called him when he was winning. Frank would sell fights that way, to bigger boxers who didn't want to be bothered with a kid. "Fast as hell and stringy strong." And he had been, still was, he thought—he had the Gold Gloves to prove it. He slid his hands under Frank's armpits, lifted him out of bed, and eased him in the chair, making sure he would stay up straight.

"Does he have a coat?" Blakely asked. The nurse handed him one and between the two of them they got Frank's arms through the sleeves. He thought of Jennifer when she was small, her strong, stubborn arms, never easy to dress.

The nurse tucked a heavy blanket around Frank's knees. "Anything else? Coffee? Hot soup? Skis?"

Blakely chuckled. "He can use my hat," he said while pulling a wool winter cap from his pocket and tugging it onto Frank's head. "Thank you."

He pushed the wheelchair into the hall and down to the double door that led into the courtyard. A small toothless woman sat at the door smiling. She mumbled something to Blakely.

"Excuse me?" he asked.

"Don't worry about Lou-Lou," a voice behind him said. "I've never met a more aptly named human being." It was another nurse, a young black woman. She flashed Blakely a grin and he pressed his lips together, closing a smile around his false teeth.

"A man could go blind looking at that smile," he said.

She fluttered her hand at him and laughed. "You come here to pick up women?"

"I was doing pretty well with Lou-Lou until you interrupted." They both laughed. He stuck out his hand. "Blakely. Please'd to meet you, ma'am."

"Don't you dare ma'am me, Mr. Blakely."

"Then don't mister me. Those shiny whites have a name to go with them?"

"Yes sir. They're called teeth. But you can call me Lissa."

"Well Lissa, it's very nice to meet you. Frank and I were just headed out to the courtyard. You're more than welcome to join us. As good as I am at making conversation, I simply cannot get Frank here involved."

"Mr. Blakely! That's not nice."

"It's just Blakely. And Frank here is my oldest—damn near only—friend and if I didn't make jokes about him, I might just steal a bunch of pills from Lou-Lou and call it a day. Besides, if you had known him when he was still talking, you'd know he can dish with the best of them."

"Did he do that to you?" She pointed at the cut above his eye.

"Frank? No. Even before all this he was gentle as a mouse." He rubbed his eyebrow. "On-the-job hazard."

She cocked her head to one side and stared at him. When she righted herself, she said, "I think I'll join you out there. Just let me get my jacket."

"Sounds like a dream. We'll be walking the path." Blakely reached by Lou-Lou and pressed the handicap button. "Excuse me, ma'am."

The courtyard was small, maybe a little bigger than the gym, and there was one sidewalk that wound around the outside, close to the building.

"Pretty girl, eh, Frank?" Blakely started the wheelchair in a clockwise path around the courtyard. "Just don't mention it to Red Eddie. I could kill him, Frank, just for being stupid and proud. And for Jennifer." He let go of the wheelchair and put the hood of his jacket up. It was supposed to be spring, but the weather was making that hard to believe.

"Thing is, he's a good fighter, Frank. Not great yet, but he's a got a helluva reach and those skinny arms end in anvils. Stringy strong."

He thought about Jennifer, hanging from Red Eddie's arm, and then about himself at twenty and her mom hanging from him and he wondered how much of those two things were the same.

"You gotta keep moving if you're gonna stay warm." He turned his head at Lissa's voice.

"That's what Frank used to tell me. Or sort of." He offered his best Puerto Rican accent. "*Gotta keep moving if you wanna stay alive, kid.* That's close, right?"

She took off her mittens and held them in her armpits. From her pocket she pulled a butterfly and some triple antibiotic.

"Old friends," he nodded at the Band-Aid. She rubbed the ointment into his skin. "I'm a boxer," he said. "Or I guess I used to be."

She pulled the paper from the back of the strip and creased it over the cut. "You sure got gentler hands than Frank here." She smiled and put on her big mittens to match her big coat and big hat.

"You look like my daughter," he said.

"You have a black daughter?"

He laughed. "No. I mean, you remind me of her. When she was little. She would beg to go out and play in the snow and I would spend twenty minutes getting her into her coat and boots and whatever and they would be huge on her, too big, so she could only totter, and we'd get out in the snow and it wouldn't be but three minutes and she'd be begging for hot chocolate back inside."

"Sounds like my daughter," she said.

"You have a daughter?" Blakely watched as she looked down at her hands and rubbed her mittens together. He thought of boxing mitts, banging and slapping the gloves, the explosive sound of cowhide on cowhide, the act of convincing yourself that this was a good idea. "I mean. Well. Hell, I'm just an old man—I can't gauge age for anything. How old?"

"Her? Four. Me? Nineteen. How old is your daughter?"

"Twenty. No. Twenty-one."

"You don't remember?"

"I was a boxer, right? And a drunk to boot. It's amazing Frank's not pushing me. Right Frankie?" He clapped his hands on his friend's shoulders. "I wasn't around much. I try to be around now though. Try to change the things I can. But back then— anyway, it's hard to keep track."

"But when you were around, you always brought her back inside for hot chocolate right away? Because my baby's daddy does that—gives her anything she wants when he shows up. Drives me nuts."

"No, I didn't. I made her stay." He grunted. "And we're still locked in a battle of wills to this day. Damn hot chocolate."

She laughed. "Well good for you. Kids need to hear no."

∞

"I don't think you should be seeing Red Eddie anymore." He was standing in Jennifer's kitchen, still wearing his coat and gloves. He had left his hat with Frank.

"I don't think you should be telling me what to do." She filled a plain metal teapot and set it on the stove. The burner clicked and lit and she sat back down at the small table.

His greatest strength as a fighter had been his ability to read his opponent, to watch for the moment when they started to wear down or favor one side. Then, bam, he struck like a snake. It was the art of precision and now, here, sweat forming at his hairline, he felt like he was throwing haymakers in the dark.

"He's dangerous. He's mean and hateful and explosive. All that adds up to dangerous."

She opened up a magazine to the middle pages. "You would know, wouldn't you?" she snapped.

She had picked up the snakebite from him. He looked down at her from where he was leaned against the countertop. She was rail thin and pale as her mother.

"That was a long time ago."

"So people change then?" He couldn't tell if it was a defense of Red Eddie or an honest question.

"I hope so." He toed a tear in the linoleum. "I've changed. I think so anyway."

He'd been thinking about it a lot. The last part of the program had been the hardest. Making amends. Taking personal inventory. Coming to know God as he understood Him. Which was hard—he'd been trying to read through the Bible and gotten hung up in the time of the judges. The wrath of God. The powerful right hand. He'd always seen God as a boxer, a real heavyweight, who wouldn't let anybody knock Him—or His people— down. It was how Blakely understood God and it was how he understood himself, he thought. But there wasn't much room to be gentle. Or to forgive. "Or maybe it's God who has changed me," he said.

"Don't bring that shit in here," she snorted.

"What?"

"That Bible-banging bullshit. I can handle all your recovery talk and all this trying to make amends for being such a shitty dad, but don't go talking about God changing you. That doesn't happen."

"How do you know that?"

"God doesn't just reach down and deliver people. You taught me that. You work and run and train and spar and *then* you become a great boxer. God doesn't just bestow that on people. And he doesn't just change people. No matter how much you want to believe it."

"So people don't change then?" This time he was asking her.

Her jaw loosened. "I don't know." She stood up from the table to pull the pot off the stove. "How the hell am I supposed to know? Did mom ever change? No. Always a liar. And now you're the one asking me. How should I know when no one ever taught me?" She poured water over a teabag and stirred it in with a plastic spoon.

He took off a glove and wiped the sweat on his forehead. She sounded just like her mother. They

sounded just like he and her mother used to,
shouting and shoving and waking all the neighbors.

"I've said I was sorry. I can't do anything else
than that." *The courage to change the things I can.*
He crossed the small kitchen and wrapped his arms
around her shoulders. Her stiff spine softened
before she broke his hold, picked up her tea and sat
back at the table.

∞

"What'd you call me down here for?" Red
Eddie was wet from the sleet falling outside, but his
hair maintained its perfect part.

Blakely was sweeping the ring. He pointed
across the gym. "You need to pay for the mirror."

"You called me down here to tell me that? You
could have said it on the phone. Then I could have
told you to go to hell. I'm not paying for no mirror."

Blakely draped himself over the end of the
broom. "Who do you think you are?" It came out
like a sigh.

"I'm Red Eddie, old man." He threw his hands
from his pockets, palms out, arms stretched wide.
Then he pointed at Blakely. "Who the hell do you
think *you* are?"

"An old man, I guess."

"Sure as shit you are." Red Eddie took a step toward the ring and shot his chin at Blakely. "Just look at yourself."

Blakely saw himself across the room, in the broken mirror, leaning hard against his broom-cane. He had seen himself in that mirror a hundred times, young and virile, unstoppable. Now—his shoulders stooped, his scalp showing through his wispy hair, his eyes heavy and dark—he just looked tired. He was tired of being tired. He tossed the broom under the bottom rope. "Prove it," he breathed.

"What'd you say?"

Blakely cleared his throat. "Prove it. Your attitude. Your supremacy. Prove you're the better man. Prove your superiority, you racist son of bitch." The whisper spun into a growl as Blakely grinded his teeth.

"You wanna go rounds with Red Eddie?"

"Yeah." He hopped up and down on the canvas and shook out his arms. "And I also want you to stop calling yourself Red Eddie."

"Alright old man. Let me get my gloves," Red Eddie turned toward the lockers.

"No gloves. Fisticuffs. True pugilists."

"You don't know what you're getting yourself into." Two quick steps and a slide through the ropes and Red Eddie was in the ring.

"Let's have a clean fight," Blakely said. "Nothing below the belt." A smile crept across his lips. His heart pounded and his fingers felt sharp and tight. "And remember: Protect yourself at all times."

Red Eddie didn't waste a minute, ape-swinging his simian arms around, two quick hooks, one to Blakely's right ear and one to his side. Blakely almost went down, feeling his knees bend under the weight of his body.

"How you like that, Grandpa Glassjaw?" Red Eddie's tic tac teeth gleamed in the fluorescent light.

He was able to get his fists up before the next jab hit his face. "Not bad, kid," he huffed. He knew his reach was too short to get a decent shot on the kid's body. He bided his time, taking blows off his forearms and the sides of body.

Red Eddie landed a good right hook that felt like it may have broken a rib, but Blakely kept his hands up, taking the blows, waiting for the right moment. He fended off another right hook only to take a left jab to his gut. The air went out of him and he lost his stance.

"You gonna buckle already, you old tomato?" Red Eddie sneered.

Blakely reached out to Red Eddie and wrapped him up. He could feel the kid's breath on his neck, their sweat mixing, their violence quelled for a moment. It was his favorite part of a fight—the clinch—the moment of peace in the midst of fury. It was the moment he had been waiting for. He slid his arm down the kid's side and Red Eddie let him, assuming he would fall. Red Eddie extended his arms, palms up, beckoning cheers from empty chairs. It gave Blakely just enough time to strike, a quick, heavy blow to the kidney, stringy strong.

Red Eddie grabbed his side and stumbled to his right. He dropped to his knees, groaning, propped up with one arm, the other holding his side.

"You stay away from my daughter," he snarled.

Red Eddie looked up from the mat. "Or what?" he exhaled.

Blakely looked at him and it felt as if he was looking through him. Past the pomade and the tiny mustache, past the bared teeth and bravado, the anger and the fear. He saw a kid, flat on the canvas, a brawler busted trying to outswing an old stylist. He had been that kid. Probably still was.

He reached his hand down and Red Eddie flinched. "I'm not gonna hit you, kid." He grabbed

Eddie's arm, the spot Jennifer had swung from earlier, and lifted him off the mat. He looked the kid in the eyes, saw the mix of fear and rage and bewilderment. He thought of God as he understood Him, the twelfth step, the spiritual awakening.

"Just don't give me a good reason to hit you again."

The Tender Kind

Luke Hawley

Paul Dudrey

1. I'm not the ten-der kind, Hir - sute and lea-ther skin.
2. My sand - pa-per hands Rough against the smooth-ness of your skin,

But the soft-ness in your eyes warms the win-ter in my wind
What we've done a thou-sand times is now a re-ve-la-tion.

When I wan-der out in to the cold It's your ea-sy voice that
When the whole world's shift-ing un-der-neath There's a still-ness in the

calls _____ me home. _____ Paint a heart in the
bed in which we sleep. _____

The Tender Kind

Painting Elephants

The front page of the Variety section had an
article about elephants that were trained to paint
pictures. The article said that when logging was
outlawed in Thailand, the elephants found
themselves unemployed and, since they themselves
were the ones that helped cut down all the forests,
they were also homeless. So they started doing
tricks to pay rent at conservation centers. Throwing
darts. Taking people's hats off. And painting
pictures. Each elephant painted a different picture: a
vase of flowers, a climbing vine—and a self-
portrait, from what must have been the most self-
aware elephant.

Margery spread the newspaper out across the
table. She stood up and walked to the junk drawer
next to the stove, pulling out a roll of masking tape.
She shuffled back to the table and taped down the
paper along the sides and at the corners. When the
paper was spread smooth, she walked into the living
room and got a basket out from under one of the
end tables. From the basket, she took a tin of paints,
a sheet of paper, a couple brushes. She kept baskets
full of art supplies and books and music for her
grandchildren. She returned to the kitchen, grabbed
an old plate from the cupboard, filled a plastic cup
with water and sat back down at the table.

She had been an art major when she met Bill.
She spent long hours in front of an easel painting
coniferous forests and fields of flowers and

mountain-peaked horizons. Bill had come to her
burly, hirsute, and quiet, the wilderness she had
been trying to paint all along. They took a trip to
Canada, her sitting next to him in the cab of his
truck. They camped along the border, cooking their
meals over a fire, pitching their tent under the
canopy of ancient trees. When they arrived home,
she had washed her brushes clean, turning her eye
to sculpting home and family.

She popped the lids off of the paints and poured
them one by one onto the plate. She dabbed the
brush in the water and spread the bristles out on the
newspaper, twisting the handle of the brush in the
fingers of her left hand. Then she undid the top
three buttons of her shirt and placed her right hand
over her left breast, kneading the flesh, searching
for what she knew she would find.

Margery began to paint, dipping into the water
and twirling out one color, pushing the bristles of
the brush into the newspaper, picking a new color.

The phone rang and Margery looked to the
corner of the kitchen where the cordless sat on its
stand. She let the machine get it. It was Bill:

*Hi honey. Just checking in. You're probably
gone to the store or something, so maybe it's
too late, but if not, would you remember pick
me up some beer? And Cheerios. I'm working
late again tonight, but maybe you'll manage to*

stay up long enough for me to see you. I love you.

Margery smiled. Almost thirty years since she had quit art school, and he still ended every phone call the same way.

She looked down at the paper. The mix of colors was beginning to take form. She rinsed out the brush and dipped it into the red paint. She watched as her hand moved in graceful figure eights across the pages, back and forth and then in smooth arcs, wide to start and ending in one sharp point. She looked at the colors in front of her. In the middle of an ocean of dark blues and purples and blacks and browns was the red of apples.

She stood from the table and walked to the phone, not remembering her paint-covered hands. She lifted the phone and dialed Bill at his office.

∞

It was a week before she could get in at the clinic. She brought the painting and tried to explain it to the doctor. He nodded along; she could see he was trying for understanding, but the tight corners of his mouth gave him away. She had admitted it herself: it *did* seem crazy. Bill had been hesitant to even let her bring the painting. But the doctor found the mass right where she said it would be.

"Bill?"

"Yes dear."

"Will you still … you know?"

"Will I still what?"

She looked down at her pork chop and summer squash. When they met, Bill had never eaten summer squash. She cooked it on their third date and when she set it in front of him, he made a face, now a familiar one, where his mouth smiled and his eyes frowned. He wasn't much for trying new things, but in the spirit of new love, he had eaten the squash and loved it. And she learned not to ask, just to do.

"My boobs. They're gonna look weird. Will you still—"

"Don't worry about it honey." He was focused on his plate, trying to spear a floppy slice of squash. The middle had softened too much in the butter and it kept slipping off the end of his fork.

"The left one is going to be…" She trailed off. Flat? Smooth? She could hardly picture a breast without a nipple.

"What?"

"It's going to be nippleless."

The Northwoods Hymnal, Luke Hawley

"Nippleless?" He looked up from his plate, his mouth smiling, his eyes not. He ran his forkless hand through his beard. "Is that a word?"

She laughed. "I suppose not." They had shared a bed for so long, shared this house. She was afraid now, of the length of the table between them, of his distance, of his hesitation.

He set his fork down and shook his head. "Nippleless." His smile spread to his eyes, then across the table to her. "Listen honey. Let's not worry about anything except getting you well. One step at a time, okay?"

She nodded.

"Okay?"

"Okay."

∞

The house smelled like chili. It was Monday night and the Packers were playing. She checked the crockpot, switching it to low. The light on the answering machine blinked.

Hi honey. It's me. I was just wondering if you could pick up some beer. A few of the guys from work are coming over. Get some good stuff and some cheap stuff, it's a mixed bag. Thanks babe. I'll see you tonight. I love you.

She headed towards the mudroom to get her coat, but stopped at the mirror hanging in the hallway. She looked down at her chest. All the bravery that people told her about, all the courage they swore she had, to get through the chemo and the reconstruction, and she still couldn't bring herself to look. She reached up under her shirt. Her breasts felt strange; they had never been this perky. The doctor had lifted the old one to match the new one, but she still felt off-balance—youthful and disfigured all at once.

She lifted her shirt over her head and stared. The stitches had healed, now a faint line ran through the center of her breast. It should have intersected a nipple, but the skin on the front of her breast was bare.

"It's not so bad, is it?" Her voice broke the quiet. She thought about Bill, his hands searching her body and finding something entirely different, but familiar.

She dropped her hands and let her breasts hang naturally. She cocked her head to the left, trying to find the right perspective. She looked at herself, at the extra skin on her face, the elasticity not what it used to be, at her tummy, her once perfect navel, her now perfect breasts. She put her arms out in front of her, looking at the skin on the backs of her arms. She moaned—Frankensteinian—crossing her eyes and twisting her face.

She giggled and pulled her shirt back down. She grabbed a plate from the kitchen and the paints from the living room. Upstairs, she undressed in front of the mirror, still staring, trying to resolve the dissonance of past and present. She spread out the paints and brushes and paper in front of the mirror and began to paint.

It came easier this time, the colors and the lines and the shapes. She was the madcap doctor, flipping switches and mixing paints, laughing at her flesh depicted in greens and browns, her hair yellow as it had been in her youth, her eyes big and blue. For the center of her right breast she chose a deep purple. Margery looked at the paper and back to the mirror and back at the paper. It wasn't quite right. She looked back to the mirror and filled the tip of the brush with more purple. In the heart of the blank canvas of her left breast, she painted a small, purple circle.

∞

The liquor store was busy with pregame patrons. She grabbed a couple cases of beer and a bottle of wine for herself and made her way to the front of the store.

"Hey you!"

She turned around.

"It's so good to see you!" It was her neighbor, Shirley. "How are you feeling?" Shirley stuck her bottom lip out as far as it would go. She was melodramatic, a small, spunky woman, whose face functioned as a mime, exaggerating everything for effect. Margery found her energy exhausting and her volume almost unbearable, but she welcomed her sympathy.

"Pretty good for now. The chemo's all done. Just the radiation left."

"Oh." Shirley frowned. "That was the toughest part for Charlie. Of course, it would be tough for any man to get his you-know-what sun burnt." She spoke into the side of her hand for you-know-what, but her volume didn't change.

Margery smiled—Bill's mouth smile. "I've heard the burn can be bad. I actually took to chemo pretty well, so I'm kind of just waiting for radiation to knock me out."

Shirley frowned and nodded. Then her eyes lit up. "But hey! Let me get a look at them." She took Margery by the shoulders, straightened her back, and stared at her chest. "This will never do!" She unzipped Margery's coat and spread it to each side of her body, as if she was looking to the back of a closet. Margery gasped and looked over the racks of wine, hoping that no one was watching them.

"My my my my my." Shirley shook her head, putting an open hand over her mouth, and widened her eyes.

Margery closed her coat and zipped it all the way, not from shame, but surprise.

"Honey. You shouldn't cover those. You should flaunt them. I *have* to get the name of this doctor from you. Charlie has taken to his changes pretty hard, what with the little pills and all, and I thought maybe I'd get some work done and see if I could get his mind off of him and onto me."

"You're gonna get work done?" It sounded so strange; it almost struck Margery as funny: Where did that phrase come from?

Shirley tossed her long, dyed hair back over shoulder and laughed. "Honey. If he can do for me what he did for you, I'll pay him anything he wants."

Margery laughed. "It's Dr. Duncan you want then. In the city. I don't think anyone here even does it."

"Not that well, they don't!"

"So you're really gonna ... for Charlie?"

Shirley spoke into the back of her hand again. "Not just for Charlie dear. For me, too. I get tired of looking at them just hanging there."

Margery thought of Bill. "You think he'll like it then?"

Shirley laughed, shrill as a fire alarm. "Charlie? Of course he'll like it. What man wouldn't?"

∞

At home, Margery emptied the cases into the fridge and double-checked the chili before going back upstairs to their room. She walked into her closet and thumbed through her clothes, searching. She found a V-necked sweater that she hadn't worn in a decade. Her hands went to her waist, her thumb and index finger spreading apart to measure her new size. Chemo does come with some perks, she thought. She smiled at *perks* and slipped the sweater over her head. In the mirror, she shifted the sweater, pulling it down and back up again, until she heard the door.

"Bill?" She made her way down the hall. She heard him scuffling in the kitchen, the fridge door opening, the crack of a can. At the sound of the television, she made her way down the stairs. "Bill?"

"Hey Margie." His baritone sounded slow and tired. "I'm in here."

She pulled down on the front of her sweater and walked through the kitchen to the living room. He was sitting in his recliner, his back to her. As she made her way around the chair, the doorbell rang. She yanked the front of the sweater up and went to answer the door.

∞

By the fourth quarter, Margery knew it would be tonight. The Packers were up by ten and Bill was laughing more than he was drinking. The year before at Thanksgiving, they had been blown out and he'd put down a case by himself. She stretched her arms over her head and let out an exaggerated sigh. "Well, boys. It looks like this one is in the bag. I think I'll head to bed." A chorus of grunts and goodnights sounded around the room. Margery stood up from her chair, walked the long way around the couch to Bill's recliner, and kissed him on the cheek.

When she reached the bedroom, she turned the television on. She lowered the volume. If the Packers found a way to blow a two score lead in five minutes, Bill would come to bed angry and everything would be ruined.

She found a lighter in the nightstand and lit every candle in the room. Margery was used to setting the mood. She could count on one hand the number of times in thirty years that Bill had gone above and beyond to be romantic. When they were first married, it had bothered her and she had let

him know. He responded with flowers and a shrug
of his shoulders. "Is this romantic?" She laughed
now, thinking about it, about the look on his face,
the bewilderment.

She turned off the light and the room seemed to
swell and shrink in the glow of candles and
television. She watched as the quarterback knelt to
let the clock run down. She found the remote and
turned the television off. The game would be over
in seconds. The house would clear out fast. She
walked into her closet and pulled her sweater over
her head. The rest of her clothes followed and she
tiptoed across the room and slid into bed, pulling
the comforter up to her neck.

The stairs creaked under Bill's slow stagger.
She heard him reach the landing and turn left into
the bathroom. Beneath the sheets, she felt the
smooth skin across the front of her breast and
thought again of Frankenstein's monster; his
translucent skin and big scared heart.

She reached across her body and turned on the
lamp. From the vanity, she took two small paint-
brushes and the paint that she had forgotten to take
downstairs. She stood in front of the mirror,
thinking about elephants and pleased audiences. She
carefully sketched the emblem in the air, making
sure it would look backwards in the mirror. She
chose a yellow-gold and dipped the brush into the
container. At the center of her left breast, where the
skin was smooth, she outlined an oval *G*. The

second brush she dipped in a bold green and finished the insignia, filling in the outline of the letter. The door opened behind her and when she turned to face her husband, she laughed, feeling both young and old, rebuilt and brand new.

All the Winter Long

Luke Hawley   Paul Dudrey

1. Just be - cause ___ he shares your bed does not mean you're
2. Has your burn - ing heart grown cold? Have you found your -

not sleep - ping a - lone. I have seen the sad - ness in your
self far a - way from home? Grow - ing bit - ter all the win - ter

eyes I have felt the weight of your hollow bones. How can you not be
long. Cer - tain that the spring will ne - ver come, How can you not be

___ sink - ing ___ low? ___ This is not how it's sup - posed to be
___ think - ing ___ oh ___

All the Winter Long

Almond Bark

"Whoever invented almond bark is a genius." The microwave beeps and my sister grabs two oven mitts off the counter. She stabs the door latch on the microwave and the door springs open. She reaches into the microwave and pulls out a glass measuring bowl full of melted brown chocolate.

"Seriously. Genius."

She carries the bowl across the kitchen to the far counter. A sheet of wax paper has been laid out across the Formica. She sets the bowl on the counter and opens the cupboard overhead. It is full of sugar. White sugar, raw sugar, brown sugar, powdered sugar. Other sweet things too. Chocolate chips, butterscotch chips, cherry chips, chocolate chunks, vanilla chips, a bag of M&Ms, assorted colors of sprinkles.

I open the refrigerator. A half-gallon of milk. A package of juice boxes for my niece. Ketchup, ranch dressing, Worchester sauce. Diet soda. Diet Coke, Diet Dr. Pepper, Diet Mountain Dew. I push the cans to the side of the fridge, searching for something sweet to drink, something that would come out of my sister's cabinets. I spy a dark can at the back of the fridge and pull it past all the diets. Coke Zero. It will have to do.

I crack the lid and watch my sister dump a bag of gummy bears into a chocolate ocean. She is blinking more than usual, tensing the muscles around her eyes. I should warn her about crow's feet, but I'll save it for mom.

"I don't know how you do it," I remark.

She looks up from stirring. "Do what?"

"Run marathons on sugar and diet soda."

"I do not!" She laughs and I believe the sound of it. It's nice to hear her laugh so loud. It's our way, the loud laugh.

"You do. It's not a criticism." I make this part clear. I know about subtext and intentions. "I'm impressed. I can't run three miles and I basically eat potatoes." I think about Christmas dinner tomorrow and the mountains of mashed potatoes and all that sweet potato casserole.

Her laugh trails off to a sigh. She is gone again, crinkling her eyes, grinding her teeth, drowning gummi bears in almond bark, pulling bodies from the mixing bowl, laying them out on wax paper. I dip my hand into a bowl full of chocolate-covered pretzels.

"Wait!" She thrusts a red Christmas tin at me. "Try this." The tin has a large evergreen on the front. For a moment I wonder why evergreens don't lose their leaves. I have lived in the North all my life. Winter would be an awful black and white without that deep green breaking up the horizon.

I open the tin and remove what looks like a ball of chocolate. My sister waits, watching me, half of her bears floating face-down in chocolate. Her skin stretches across the loom of her cheekbones, as if her eternal happiness rests on my opinion of her snacks. I make a mental note to kill my brother-in-law.

I take a bite of the chocolate, which softens on impact with my tongue. The inside is almost bready, sweet and doughy. Of course: Chocolate covered cookie dough. I nod my head, the half moon of uneaten chocolate and dough still lifted to my mouth, my free hand cupped under my chin, catching bits of hardened chocolate before they fall to the floor.

"Good." My mouth is full and I push the extra food into my cheek. "It's really good." It drives my wife nuts that I keep food in my cheeks and talk while I eat. I've explained that in my family, you have to get a word in whenever you can, at any cost, but she just shakes her head.

She is already at Mom and Dad's, starting the turkey, picking up the house. I picture my tiny daughter rolling around on the kitchen floor, playing with assorted kitchen utensils. It's just something my mom does, give kids utensils for toys.

My sister has finished laying out the gummy bears. She is filling the bowl with more almond bark. She pops the latch on the microwave door and puts the mixing bowl in and starts the time. It's too late but I try anyway: "Shouldn't we be leaving?"

She turns from the microwave to look at me. She is crying, holding the wooden spoon, hair tangled in chocolate, tears cutting rivulets down her cheeks, her nose a delta, her skin alluvial. Lately it comes like this, these fits of despair, out of nowhere. "Hey. Hey." I try my best to sound like I understand, but I don't, and I'm nervous that I brought it all on with the comment about marathons and sugar and diet soda. "It's alright. We can wait a little while longer. Can I load up your stuff for you?"

Movement is my default when I can't make sense of a situation. When my sister called to tell me about my brother-in-law, that he had lost his job again, neglected to tell her again—this time for three weeks—and she doesn't know where he goes or what he does all day, and sometimes all night, and what is she supposed to do and she can't be married to him anymore but what about little Grace and seriously what is wrong with him—I hung up the phone and moved every piece of furniture in our apartment to a new spot. But the apartment is oblong, the rooms all weird shapes and angles, and the furniture was either too big or too small so when my wife arrived home from work, I had moved our bedroom to the living room and most of the living room furniture to the kitchen and the dining room table was set up where our bed had been. She dropped her workbag and I saw she was going to ask, but then I just sat down, right down on that big recliner clogging up our galley kitchen and I cried. For my sister, and for my niece too, but also because it wasn't how things were supposed to go.

"I just need to finish dipping these peanut butter cracker sandwiches and then I think I'll be ready to go." She wipes her eyes with the back of the hand that holds the wooden spoon. A mess of her hair catches in the scoop of the spoon, but she doesn't realize it, so when she pulls the bowl out of the microwave, she stirs long hairs into the mix. I will skip the peanut butter cracker sandwiches. "All the stuff that is going to Mom's is in the front entryway. Would you really carry it out for me? That would be so great." She smiles, but it's mostly sad. She turns back around to her bowl of chocolate and the wax paper counter.

I walk through the dining room and into the living room and turn the knob of the front door in my fist. I pull the door open and there, in the entryway, is what my sister has been doing for the three days since my brother-in-law left: stacks of Christmas tins, red and green and white and silver, covered in pictures of trees and snowflakes and laughing Santas and Ho Ho Hos and reindeer and stockings hung on fireplaces. I open the first one. White-chocolate pretzels. I open another and toss a piece in my mouth. Chocolate popcorn. I open a third: Rice Krispies' Treats. A fourth: gummi worms. A fifth: Chex Mix, I think. Sixth: Cheese puffs. Not good. I skip the rest and wade through the tins, clanging like cymbals against my legs. In the back of the entryway, I see what looks like a whole honey-glazed bone-in ham covered in chocolate. And a dining room chair. And her entire drawer of silverware. Also, a hairdryer. And in the corner a small mattress, and on that small mattress, my sleeping niece. All drenched in chocolate. On a stack of tins in front of me, covered in a hard shell and drizzled in white chocolate, like the pretzels, a piece of paper. I fold it in half and watch the chocolate spiderweb, cracking into a thousand pieces. I can make out her name and her husband's name and an official looking seal.

I take high steps back to the front door, trying my best not to disrupt the precarious order of tins. I don't want to wake my niece. I crane my neck around the threshold and call back to the kitchen.

"All of this goes?"

"Yeah—can you just throw it in your truck?" It makes sense now, why she had me come over in the truck. I hear the microwave beep. I should remind her that the little peanut butter cracker sandwiches are the last item to be dipped, but I know that it will take me a while to move all this stuff. And I am glad to have the work to do.

Murder in the Heart, Murder in the Hand

Luke Hawley

Joe Mann

1. Don't you for - get ____ You're the one who
And now I wait ____ with ____ ba - ted
2. My mo - ther swears ____ I ____ have no
But you gave me ____ This ____ sweet ____

prom - ised ____ that you'd love me 'til you died.
breath, babe, for that mo - ment to ar - rive.
sense, the ____ way I fell for you.
ba - by, ____ What was I sup - posed to do?

When you swore that you loved ____ me ____

Murder in the Heart, Murder in the Hand

Fifty-Seven Ways to Kill a Rat

One: A Bucket and the Natural World

"It's perfect!"

"I knew you'd love it."

"I do I do I do I do I do! It's exactly what I wanted."

"We're officially country people."

"It's – It's – What's the word I'm looking for?"

"Pastoral?"

"No."

"Bucolic."

"No no no. It starts with an I."

"Idyllic?"

"Idyllic! That's it! You totally know me better than anyone else on this earth."

"And you haven't even seen the kitchen yet. It's just through there."

"With a little breakfast nook and everything!"

"I thought you'd like that. I was thinking I could find like a booth from an old diner or something. Don't you think that would go great in there?"

"Hmm. Maybe. Or! One of those old rectangular tables that has semi-circle leaves on each side—you know what I mean? It's a rectangle, but then it can be a circle too?"

"I know what you mean. I don't know that it will fit in there. Not like a diner booth anyway."

"I guess."

"You guess? You don't like the diner booth idea?"

"That's not it. I just. I don't want to upset the id—what was the word?"

"Idyllic?"

"Right! The idyllic nature of things, I don't want to upset it. I want to keep it in tact. I don't want to ever think of the city when we're home."

"And diners make you think of the city?"

"Yes."

"They make me think of country truck stops."

"I guess. But I'm thinking about that place in St. Paul. Downtown. The place that's like a train car."

"Mickey's?"

"Yes! Mickey's! It's like you're here to clean up after all my lost thoughts."

"It happens with pregnancy, doesn't it?"

"Mom calls it pregnancy brain. She was telling me about when she was pregnant with my sister—Oh My God!"

"What! What?"

"Did you see it—Oh my God—Oh my God!—Get it! Right there—under the cabinet!"

"Will you stop yelling? What are you yelling about?"

"I'm pointing right at it—you don't see it? A mouse!"

"Oh. Yeah. I see it now."

"Kill it then!"

"Stop yelling. We don't need to kill it."

"Where are you going?!"

"Just—lower your volume—hold on—it's in here somewhere. Ah-ha! Got it."

"The mouse?"

"No. Not the mouse. Yet. Come here, little fella. Come to papa. It's gonna be just fine. I'm just gonna—gotcha!"

"You killed him?"

"Uncover your eyes. C'mon. Nothing to be scared of, just a little country mouse. You want to see him?"

"I do not want to see him! Just kill him already!"

"Stop yelling. He's not getting out of this bucket. I'll just go let him out in the yard."

"He'll come back in the house, won't he?"

"I'll put him out at the end of the drive."

"Just kill him already."

"He'll probably die out there on his own anyway."

Five: The Old-Fashioned Way

"You don't use cheese?"

"You can use cheese. Peanut butter works better though. It's harder to get off the trap. Mice are pretty smart. And pretty hard to catch. It's a battle of odds right now. If we put out enough traps, we should be able to take care of the problem before it gets out of control."

"Out of control?"

"Before they breed. Once they breed—well, let's say the phrase shouldn't be *like rabbits*, it should be *like mice*. They take over. Closets, dark corners. They get in the walls—then you really have trouble. Then you have to call someone."

"Shouldn't we just do that now?"

"No way. Too expensive. It's not a real problem yet. I'll be able to get them all. Don't worry about it."

"They need to be gone before the baby comes. I'm gonna start having nightmares about hoards of mice carrying our baby off to some underground lair."

"They don't live underground."

"Whatever. Some secret lair. In the walls."

"The baby can't fit in the walls. There's definitely not enough room."

"I said nightmares right? Anything can happen in nightmares."

"I guess. But I wouldn't worry about it. Peanut butter and old-fashioned traps should do the trick."

"Should?"

"Will. It'll do the trick. I promise."

"Okay. I trust you."

"Thanks. I can hear the confidence in your tone."

"Honey! I do trust you. They just gross me out. And they need to be gone before the baby gets here."

"They'll be gone."

"What would I do without you to take care of me?"

"Be carried off by mice to an underground lair?"

Twelve: The Ruth Goldberg Machine

"This is just like that game!"

"What game?"

"Mousetrap."

"The mousetrap? It's not a game, babe. It's just an elaborate mousetrap."

"Not *this* mousetrap. The Mousetrap Board Game—you probably never played it. Of course you never played it, you spent all your free hours milking cows—"

"Not just milking cows. We didn't just have dairy."

"I know honey. I just meant—we bought it because we saw it on TV. You probably just never saw it—it was just a dumb game."

"What are you talking about?"

"Mousetrap. It's a board game. You set up this elaborate device with plastic slides and a marble and a scale, I think, and at the end you catch a mouse."

"That's the game? What's the point? It doesn't sound like a game. What's the game?"

"Well that's not the whole game. We just only ever set up the trap. It took long enough for God's sake. I can't even think of what the actual rules were, like what the point was, or how you won or anything. I just remember the device. That's why I said something. Because it reminds me of this."

"Are you ready?"

"Ready for what? We're just waiting, right?"

"Yeah. But that guy living in the closet is extra dumb. All it'll take is a little peanut butter and he'll come right out."

"Then what happens?"

"He'll pull on the rope there—the end'll be covered in peanut butter. He's so fat he'll just keep at it. And while he's at it, the rope will pull on the ruler, which'll knock the baseball into the laundry basket. When the basket drops—Wait! Shh. Shh. Here he comes."

"He's going for it!"

"Shh. Of course, he's going for it. There— there!—the ruler—the baseball—the basket pulling on the blinds—the book falling of the sill and knocking the—Got him! it worked!"

"It worked! We got him!"

"*We* got him?"

"Well you know what I mean. We caught him. In your machine."

"*I* caught him in *my* machine."

"Right. You caught him in your machine. Because you wouldn't let me help you build it."

"You're nine months pregnant—"

"So I'm useless? Is that it? I'm useless? Why don't you just say it?"

"Jesus. You're not useless—"

"What have I told you about taking the Lord's name in vain?"

"Sorry. It's just—You're acting a little crazy."

"Now I'm crazy? I could kill you sometimes. First I'm useless and now I'm crazy?"

"Hold on now. I never called you useless."

"But crazy is okay?"

"I just said you're *acting* a *little crazy*."

"I can read between the lines."

"Whatever. I'll just get rid of it and give you some time."

"Time to what?"

"Cool off or whatever."

"Now you're just gonna leave? Here we are having a discussion and you're just gonna leave?"

"A discussion?"

"An argument. A fight. I don't care what you want to call it. You can't just leave in the middle of it. In my family we learned to talk things out."

"Not in my family."

"Your family is crazy."

"Now my family is—whatever. I'm gonna get rid of the mouse and I'll be back in a while."

"What if I go into labor?"

"You won't if you just calm the hell down. I'll be back in an hour."

Seventeen: Hospital Bag

"Ohmygodohmygodohmygod!He'scominghe's cominghe'scoming!"

"Okay. Alright. Okay. Just breathe."

"What do you think I'm trying to do?"

"Right. Just breathe. Put your shoes on. I'll grab the bag and the keys and we'll be on our way— Where's the bag? Where did you put the bag?"

"Where did I put the bag? Where did you put the bag?"

"I didn't put it anywhere. You've been cleaning the house nonstop for three days and I can't find anything that I put anywhere. I don't know where my glasses are. I don't know where my wallet is. They don't ask for proof of identification when you have a baby do they? Shit. Where is that stupid bag?"

"There! Right there!"

"Where? What are you pointing at?"

"There! There! There!"

"It's not over there. Wait. I remember I saw it— Here. Here it is. I got it."

"There! There!"

"I have it. Right here. What are you pointing at?"

"Theretheretheretherethere!"

"Will you stop yelling! What are you—?"

"A mouse! He's coming for my—he's in my—"

"Your purse? Which one? There are like twenty purses here."

"It's not a purse—it's a clutch! There! The red leather!"

"I see it. Hold on. I can just—my hands are just pretty full—I'll just drop this—whatever it's called—handbag?"

"That's our hospital bag!"

"Sorry. Now it's a weapon of mouse destruct-tion. Get it?" *Squish.* "Got him. There. See? Now let's get to that hospital!"

"You just ruined two perfectly good bags."

"I thought it was a clutch."

Twenty: Indifference

"Psst. PSST!"

"Wha?"

"There's a mouse in here. I need you to get it."

"Go back to bed. There's no mouse."

"I can't go back to bed. Our son is hungry. And there is a mouse in here."

"Just—why can't you just let me sleep?"

"Why can't you ever help with anything?"

"Ever?"

"I'm sorry. It's the middle of the night. I'd like to be sleeping too. Can you please just kill the mouse?"

"The trap will get it."

"I can hear it scurrying around. If it's not caught yet, it's not going to be."

"The trap will get it. Just go back to sleep."

"I've already told you I can't."

"Then let me go back to sleep."

"You're absolutely no help."

"Stop talking in superlatives."

"In what?"

"Never mind. Just let me sleep."

"Oh sure. Go right ahead. Enjoy your sleep. Sleep like a baby. What a stupid phrase. Babies don't sleep. Babies wake up in the middle of the night and get their mamas up while their stupid dads are too lazy to do one damn thing for their mamas. How hard is it to kill a mouse?"

Snap.

"Not hard. I told you. Not hard. Just let the traps do their job and let me sleep.

"Ooh. I hate when you're right."

Twenty-four: Boiling water

"Just a minute, baby boy, just a minute. Mama's gonna have your bottle here any second now. Mama's so sorry she couldn't convince Daddy to buy a microwave. So sorry, pumpkin. The water is heating up. I know you won't have it cold. Just like your daddy won't have a country house with a microwave. But that's the key to marriage, right? Compromise? Right? Daddy goes to work all day and brings home the money and Mama doesn't complain about living without modern amenities."

"Here we go baby boy. There you are, pumpkin. Slow down, slow down. You're gonna give yourself a tummy ache. And then you're gonna give Mama a headache. Mama loves you baby boy, she just needs a break sometimes. There you go, nice and slow, drink it slow now. Daddy will be home soon. Then Mama can have a break and you can spend some time with Daddy. Who knows? Maybe he's late because he's bringing Mama a microwave. It's the only way his dinner's gonna be warm. That'll teach him. No microwave? Come home late? Cold hotdish. Those are natural consequences, sweetheart."

"Someday Mama will tell you about the natural consequences of not using protection. Or maybe she won't. Maybe Daddy will tell you. We love you baby boy, Mama loves you so much. She just didn't think it was gonna be like this. But you learn to roll with the punches. Like boiling water, just roll, over and under, over and under."

"Oh shit. Oh no. Oh no. I thought he got the last of you! You're supposed to be gone! Hold on, baby boy. Mama just has to set the bottle down for a second. Daddy said he took care of the mice, but he didn't. Mama's gonna kill him. The mouse that is. Mama's just gonna set the bottle down here. Don't cry baby boy, don't cry. Mama's gotta take care of this. Just hold on. Get out of my sink you bastard!"

"Don't cry baby boy, don't cry. Mama's not yelling at you. Just hold on a second here. Mama's just gonna grab this pot of water here. This should take care of everything. It's alright, baby boy, it's alright. Mama's just gonna dump it—Die mouse. Die!"

"Oh baby boy! Don't cry! Don't cry! Mama's got your bottle. Don't cry. Good boy, just drink up. Don't cry. Are you still crying? Is that you? Is that the bottle? What's that squealing?"

Thirty-One: Lamp

"So how long until—you know?"

"What?"

"How long? What's the wait now? It's been five weeks. It can't be that much longer."

"Are you talking about sex?"

"Yeah. What else would I be talking about?"

"I don't know."

"You don't know how long, or you don't know what else I would be talking about?"

"Either. Both. You could have been talking about the baby. You could have been asking how long until he smiles."

"Really? You really think that's what I might have been talking about? He's sleeping soundly and we're lying in bed and you think that's what I'm wondering about?"

"It would be nice if you would take more interest in him."

"More interest? Are you kidding? Don't change the subject."

"I'm serious. You just seem—preoccupied. Just lately."

"I'm working like sixty hours a week. And going to school. What more do you want from me?"

"Don't talk in super—superwhatevers."

"Superlatives."

"I want you to be interested in our baby."

"I am interested. I hold him, right? I would feed him, but I don't have the proper equipment for that."

"I know. It just seems like—it seems like I have to make you hold him. It seems like I have to force you to spend time with him."

"This is about diapers, isn't it? Look. I tried to help with diapers, but you kept looking at me like I wasn't doing it right, like I was an idiot. Like you felt sorry for me."

"I did not. I looked at you like this—like I thought it was so cute how you were trying to change his diaper."

"See? *Trying*? Stop patronizing me."

"Sorry. I'm not *trying* to patronize you."

"And you want to know the truth? It's kinda hard to be interested in him. He doesn't do anything. I try to make him laugh and he just stares at me. Or worse. He starts hollering. He's probably just a mama's boy. When he gets older I'll teach him things. How to throw a football. How to shoot a gun. That kind of stuff."

"He's not gonna want to do any of that stuff with you if you don't show interest in him now."

"Oh? So he's gonna only be interested in what you're interested in? God help him."

"At least he'll know the difference between a clutch and a purse."

"God help us all then!"

"Where are you going?"

"To make a sandwich."

"I'm trying to talk to you here."

"I'll be back. I'm just going into the kitchen. You can just keep talking. I'm sure I'll catch on when I get back. And by the way. You want me to show some interest in the baby? How about you show some interest in your husband? What am I to you anyway? A donor?"

"You're an asshole."

"Better than a hypocrite."

"A hypocrite? I hardly thin—" Smash! "What was that for?!"

"Stop yelling. You'll wake the baby."

"I'll wake the baby? You just threw a perfectly good lamp across the room for no reason!"

"Here's my reason. A perfect strike."

"Is that a mo—Get it out of here—Get it out of my room!"

"Your room?"

"You know what I mean. I thought you said you were taking care of all the mice."

"I am."

"If this is your new strategy I'm leaving."

"You're not leaving. It's not my new strategy. We don't have enough lamps for this to be my new strategy."

"Now where are you going?"

"You want me to keep it in here? I'm going to throw it out. Then I'm gonna make a sandwich."

Forty-Six: The three inch heel

"Where are you going?"

"I'm going out with the guys."

"Like hell you are. I'm going out tonight. You're staying back with the little man."

"He's sleeping right?"

"Yes."

"So I won't be gone long. He'll still be asleep when I get back."

"Are you kidding me? Are you crazy? You can't leave a six month old infant home by himself, just sleeping in his bed!"

"My parents did. And I turned out alright."

"Debatable."

"What's that supposed to mean?"

"It means that if you think you can leave a baby at home while you go out to the bar, then maybe you didn't turn out alright."

"I'm not going to the bar."

"Oh?"

"I'm going to play pool."

"And where, pray tell, does one play pool in this town?"

"[*mumble mumble*]"

"That's right. The bar. Besides, you're not going anywhere. Tonight's my night."

"And where the hell are you going?"

"The bar."

"All done up like that? You coming home tonight? Or looking for a different bed?"

"It's girl's night, asshole. We're gonna drink a bunch of wine and talk shit about men. And maybe—depending on the wine—we'll dance. Me and my beautiful lime green heels."

"Right. Good luck dancing in those."

"These? They're only three-inch. And my feet aren't swollen anymore."

"About the only part of you that's not swollen."

"You're a bastard, you know that? I'm not gonna let you ruin my night with—Oh my God! I thought you killed all those mice!"

"Just stomp it."

"In these? Oh lord oh lord oh lord! It's gonna climb my—"

"It likes your shoes."

"Kill it!"

"If you let me go out tonight."

"Screw you." *Squish.* "Sit your ass down on that couch. I need to change my shoes and then I'm going out."

Fifty-seven: Rodenticide

"This soup is awful."

"Of all the terrible things I might say about you, I could never bring myself to call you a liar."

"Well it is. I mean the chicken is good, but something in here smells like a diaper."

"Ha! A diaper. And how would you know about the smell of a diaper in the first place?"

"Very funny. Is it the rice? Did you get a bad sack of rice or something?"

"Not that I know of. And you keep eating it, so it can't be that bad. Rice doesn't go bad, does it?"

"I'm starving and there's nothing else to eat in this house besides diaper soup. And what do you mean *rice doesn't go bad*?"

"I mean I don't think it goes bad. I found a sack under the sink."

"Did you use it in this? Is that what I'm eating?"

"No. I used the rest of the good stuff."

"Are you serious? Because if I'm eating rice from like World War Two or something—"

"I'm serious. The nice thing about being married to someone as honest as you is that I don't ever feel the need to lie."

"It's not really the diaper smell. I had a bowl of wild rice soup that smelled like that once and it tasted fine. It's like a bitter taste or something."

"Can't put your tongue on it?"

"What?"

"Can't put your tongue on it? You know, like can't put your finger on it?"

"That joke was as good as this soup. Where's the baby?"

"He's at mom's. So nice of you to ask."

"I'm trying."

"Sure you are. You just want to know if you can go down to the bar without guilt tonight."

"Whatever. I don't feel guilty."

"That's what you say."

"I don't. A man needs his time away from home."

"That's all of your time."

"Excuse me for trying to make a living."

"You're excused."

"Does this mean you're going somewhere tonight? "

"Not necessarily. I might go, I might not."

"You know what we should do? Since the baby's not here? We should put out that rodenticide."

"Will you just call it rat poison? Nobody calls it rodenticide."

"That's the proper name for it."

"It's the presumptuous name for it."

'"I think you mean pretentious."

"See? You proved my point. Always correcting everything I say. Have some more soup."

"There's really nothing else to eat in this house?"

"Nope."

"Maybe you should go grocery shopping tonight."

"Maybe you should stop blowing our grocery money."

"Maybe you should stop nagging."

"Your face is twitching."

"What do you mean?"

"I mean your face is twitching. There—on the right side."

"You don't ever get twitches? Like in the corner of your eye?"

"Not like that."

"It's fine. I'll be just fine. I might just need to lie down."

"I think you mean lay down."

"I most certainly do not mean lay down. I'm just going to *lie* down here."

"It's getting worse there. The twitching."

"I know. I just—is it warm in here? I'm sweating. We can't afford to keep it this hot."

"Just lay down. You'll be fine."

"*Lie down*. I think you mean *lie down*."

"I mean whatever I damn well say. Like when I say this: It's called rat poison. Nobody calls it rodenticide. Or strychnine. It's called rat poison."

"Who said anything about strychnine?"

"Nobody."

"Can you bring me that afghan? I'm so cold."

"Cold? A second ago you were burning up."

"I am. I'm sweating. And freezing. I must be running a fever or something. And who said anything about strychnine?"

"Nobody. It's rat poison, right?"

"It *was* rat poison. Nobody uses it anymore. No one has used it since like World War Two."

"You really are an expert on everything. Any idea why they stopped using it?"

"They developed better options. Options that didn't kill people."

"Did you know that people used to take strychnine for a laxative?"

"Yes. And as a stimulant. Look at you and your trivial information!"

"It's not trivial."

"It's not trivial?"

"It's research."

"Research?"

"How to kill a rat."

"I told you I'd take care of it."

"And you did, huh? We've been here almost a year and I still wake up every morning to a rat."

"They're mice. Not rats. I can't stop shaking."
"And yet you have the energy to correct me…"

"Can you turn the heat up?"

"I thought you said we couldn't afford it."

"Fine. Get me a blanket then."

"Get it yourself."

"I can't move. I mean I can't stop shaking. But I can't get up."

"It won't be much longer then. I mean it'll get worse but relatively speaking it won't be that much longer."

"What won't be much longer?"

"First the convulsions. Then the cramps and the hypothermia. Then paralysis."

"What are you talking about?"

"First paralysis of your muscles, along with rhabdomyolysis. Did I say that right? You *do* know what that is?"

"I don't know what any of this is. You're not making any sense. Can you just get me a blanket? Can you call a doctor?"

"Rhabdomyolysis is the rapid breakdown of skeletal muscle. Did you know you can say skeletal two different ways and be right either way?

Skeletal—as in skeleton. Or skel*ee*tal, with the long E."

"Doctor. Please. Doctor."

"Anyway, rhabdomyolysis leads to kidney failure. But that's not what gets you in the end. What gets you in the end is the paralysis. Asphyxiation, actually."

"Strychnine?"

"Yes dear. Strychnine. I found it under the sink by the rice. By the way, when I said I didn't use the old rice? I was lying. And when I said I didn't need to lie to you? Well that was true. But I did. I lied because I could."

"[*mumble mumble*]"

"Something to say, dear? Let me lean in close."

"Strychnine."

"Yes. Strychnine. I told you that."

"Cliché."

"You're a bastard. You're gonna be a dead bastard soon. A pretentious bastard who's gonna be a dead bastard. I hope it makes you feel better, to be correct at the very end, to be better than me. But you can take this with you too: Your death is a

cliché. As unoriginal as you. Derivative.
Unexceptional. Hackneyed, trite, uninspired.
Commonplace."

.

What Holds Us Together

Luke Hawley

Joe Mann

What Holds Us Together

The Devolution of Man

Pete held the change of address card in his hand up to the silver numbers on the building and tried to focus his eyes. "One. Eight. Nine. Seven." He folded the card and put it back in his pocket. He picked up the bag of balls and what was left of the six-pack and walked around the back of the building. It looked like an eightplex, so he figured number 7 to be the last apartment on the right on the second floor.

From the edge of the building he counted out sixty feet, walking as straight a line as possible. He set the bag down and loosened the string. He found the fifth of Yukon Jack, lifted it to safety and then dumped the rest of the baseballs on the ground. He cracked one of the beers and gulped the first third, before refilling the can with whiskey.

Projectable. It was word they had used for him. Drafted out of high school because he threw smoke. Big frame. Good baseball body. Would fill out in time. Pete looked down at the soft paunch hanging over his belt. He filled out fine.

On a slight rise in the sod, he toed a divot into the fresh grass. The window was a good eight or ten feet up off the ground, so it wasn't quite just throwing strikes. He drank his Special Beer, a McConnell family recipe, down about halfway and set it at the back of the mound. He picked up a ball, tossed it up and down in his hand a couple of times, and put his back foot in the divot. He straightened his back, making himself as tall as possible, like O'Leary taught him.

"Nobody on. Working from the windup. This kid can bring heat, it's just a matter of where he brings it." Pete leaned back and brought his leg up. It wasn't the high kick all those rookie league coaches hated, but that was age, not choice. He brought his arm back and folded in his body, before loosing his ligaments into a mess of arms and legs. *CRACK.* The ball caromed off the plastic siding, a foot off to the left of the window. A long, straight line split the length of the white vinyl siding.

"Outside. Ball one." Pete walked to the back of the mound. The beer teetered on the grass where a resin bag ought to sit. He picked up the can, finished it off in two long pulls, and crumpled it in his hand.

He rubbed his right shoulder with his left hand. His rotator cuff had been the beginning of the end. A slight tear and his bullets turned to bowling balls and some Neanderthal with a caveman stick caught him on the jaw on a comebacker to the mound. They wired his mouth shut and tried to fix his shoulder, but he never got his fastball back. A righty who can't crack ninety is a lost link in the evolutionary chain of minor league ball.

A new ball, his fingers working the rawhide, his palms riding the seams. He stepped back into his groove, digging his loafers into the dirt. He leaned forward and rotated the ball in his hand behind his back, until his index and middle fingers found the seams. "McConnell is ready to throw. Back into the windup." He crumpled and uncrumpled and fired the ball from his hand. It clanged off the metal edge of window.

"Steee-rike one!" Pete tripped on his follow-through and wobbled in the grass. "McConnell just nicked the corner there, enough to get the call." Another beer: tapped, opened, swigged. Another ball, squeezed, rotated, gripped. He stopped at the top of his rotation. Sirens in the distance.

"You *would* call the police!" He shook the ball at the side of the apartment. "Why not just call me? We can talk this out." He slipped on the sod and kicked over the beer. "Like adults."

He picked up the beer and drank the remainder, the foam coating his beard. He regained his stance, reared back, kicked his leg high, and fired again. "Steee-rike two! We're hucking the high heat now!" Lines snaked away from the center of the glass, small shards falling down into the lawn below.

"Two strikes. That's all I got, that's all you get." Pete grabbed the canvas bag and the remaining beer and turned back towards his car.

"You can go to hell, Jezebel."

∞

That night, he had dreamt again that all his teeth were falling out. He reached a finger up to his face. Still there. In the dream, he was eating bananas. He was sitting on a playground next to a stack of bananas and every time he peeled one and bit into it, he lost a tooth. He was so angry at the bananas, but so hungry that he kept at it, peeling and biting and spitting teeth into his hands.

He brought his hand down from his mouth and rubbed it against his arm. The house was freezing. Did he leave all the windows open? Every day now is full of questions like that: Why didn't he close the windows? Where are his keys? Did he pay the electric bill? How the hell did he get home? Why was he sleeping on the love seat?

He got up and turned the crank to bring in the window, locking it in place. Eyes squinting, he groped for the thermostat and slid the dial all the way to one side.

Pete felt his stomach turn over, gurgling, like a cow drowning in mud. He lunged down the hallway, toward the bathroom, and vomited right into the bathtub. He couldn't get the seat up in time. Oh, she had trained him well. Lived alone and still put the seat down.

He ran the bath water and the combination of steam and vomit made him sick again, into the sink this time. He wiped his face with the back of his hand and looked in the mirror. His eyes hung back in his skull, swallowed by the bags underneath them. The hair on his face was speckled with white, running up into the scattered grays left on his head. Started losing his hair when he quit playing ball, another thing he couldn't get back.

In the kitchen, the coffee pot blinked 12:00 in red letters. For his 38th birthday, Laura got him a self-grinding coffee maker. The comfort of modern living, the simplicity of the technological age. No more boiling water, no more crushing beans with mortar and pestle, no more percolation. Easy living. She used to buy lingerie for his birthday.

He shook the bottle of ibuprofen kept in the windowsill above the sink. Sounded like one, but he opened the cap to find what might be the best thing that would happen to him all day: Two tablets.

"It's a start," he mumbled, a benediction for better things. He headed back to the bedroom to sleep for another hour and walked past a picture of Laura on the nightstand. She and a bunch of friends had gotten all geared up on a girls-day-out and dropped in on the glamour shots studio at the mall. It was a ridiculous picture—too much makeup and too much hair, washed out from the bright lights.

"Once a beauty queen, always a beauty queen," he mumbled.
Pete remembered Laura best in the morning, when she rolled over and kissed him with her

morning mouth, her hair all twisted, eyes half open. That was a woman, sleepy-eyed and unkempt and still capable of knocking a man out. That was the real stuff.

He cursed, coughed, and looked out at the driveway, where his car was not parked. He reached into his left pants pocket and he found his keys.

"Fantastic." He rolled his arm around at the shoulder and headed for the shower. No time for a shave, but the hot water would help his sore muscles. He remembered then as he rubbed his shoulder: the bag of baseballs, Laura's broken window, crashing a bicycle into the dumpster at Duffy's. His car must be at Laura's place. Bike first, he thought.

∞

Brake lights.

Compress the clutch. Lay off the gas. Press the brake.

No brake lights.

Ease off the clutch. Gentle on the gas.

Brake lights.

Clutch. Off the gas. Brake.

No brake lights.

This is how we make our forward progress.

Pete watched the traffic backed up on the
bridge over Charlie Creek. He was on the Schwinn.
It rode nice for an old bike. The original two-lane
beam bridge was built before the southside boom.
The city had been lobbying for years to expand the
bridge but the proposal never passed. They would
have to close the bridge during construction and the
next nearest creek crossing was out past the edge of
town. The traffic made a short commute feel long, a
smallish town seem big, a lousy job important.

He pedaled the Schwinn and headed south to
where his car was parked. He was usually with them
now, the bump and go traffic, eating a custard filled
doughnut, drinking gas station cappuccino,
scanning the newspaper in the passenger seat, and
switching the dial between morning shows. On the
way home he did the crossword puzzle. His daily
adventure. He looked down at the spokes of the
bicycle blurring into one another and wished he had
a baseball card to shove between them.

He passed through the industrial park that ran
down the middle of town and into the spit-polished
shine of the southside. He hung a right on Sycamore
and wheeled into the parking lot of Laura's
complex. The Taurus was right where he left it,
parked across two spots on the edge of the lot. He
pulled on the handbrakes and grinded to a halt. He

leaned the Schwinn against the back of the car and looked through the rear window to see if his radio is still intact.

No one steals a tape player, he thought. When he bought the Taurus he had been thinking practically. A family car, one that the three of them could take across the country. He spent all he could, signed on the line, and drove it home, shiny and maroon, him and his cheeseburger grin. She didn't like the color and the boy wanted a CD player.

Pete opened the back door and pulled the lever to fold the backseat down, sweeping the trash from the seat to the floor. He moved around to the back of the car and unlocked the trunk. As he lifted the bike up to his waist, he felt, in his lower back, the consequence of a night on the love seat. He shoved the back wheel into the back seat, found a small bungee in the utility compartment of the trunk, and hooked it under the bumper, pulling the trunk down over the front tire of the Schwinn. He walked back around to the front seat, sat down, and looked through the passenger window at the entrance to Laura's building.

A man in a pinstripe shirt and navy blazer was leaving through the front door. He took the three steps down to the sidewalk and turned into the parking lot. He was young and handsome. And vaguely familiar. Pete watched him turn back towards the apartment where a woman was waving her arms, calling his name. He watched as the two

smiled at each other, as the woman handed him a
bundle of mail, as she touched his arm. She seemed
to linger before she headed back into the apartment,
tossing her hair and showing all the teeth in her
smile. He watched the man walk all the way to his
vehicle, a white Blazer. He listened to the bass
boom as the man started the engine and heavy beats
blasted from the stereo.

∞

The traffic light in front of him changed to
yellow and Pete shifted into fifth gear and blew
through it. He kept his left hand on the bottom of
the wheel and turned the radio up with his right
hand. It was the AM band, some local sports expert
shouting about how talented the Yankees are and
when October comes calling they'll be there again.
Damn Yankees. What did they know about talent?
They bought their wins. If they knew anything
about talent their rookie ball coaches would have
turned him into what he was supposed to be. An
ace. Top of the rotation guy. Two hundred innings,
two hundred strikeouts. He could still be
throwing—half-seasons maybe—pulling in three or
four million for under a hundred innings.

The insurance company Pete worked for was
housed in a five-story office building on the
southside of town. It was one floor short of the
tallest building in town and, from the sidewalk
outside, a person could see the shame in the

building's construction, a washed-out pale brick building, sagging window frames.

He pulled into the parking garage and remembered an article he had read in the New York Times. A professor out of Texas surmised that modern men were more likely to beat or murder their wives because of the evolutionary habits of caveman. The logic was that when Wife A left Caveman A for Caveman B, Caveman A's line ended there, and the sensitive man was snuffed out by the cold hard fact of evolution. But when Wife A tried to leave Caveman B, he went out, found her, and beat her to death, and improved his power standing while attracting Wife B because he was the stronger, more aggressive male. And when Wife B tried to leave him, maybe he beat her to death too, but when Wife C tried to leave, he beat her into submission, thus the future of gender roles and wife beating was worked right into the evolutionary cycle.

It made sense that she left him. He had always been behind the evolutionary curve. He played it off by making rash decisions and insisting that he was always right. Confidence goes a long way. But now? He hadn't done a damn thing for the last twenty-five years except eat, shit, sleep, and think about all the things he'd missed out on. If Doc Brown pulled up in his Delorian and they took off 88 miles an hour into the past and he met his 18 year old self, Pete was certain he would get his flabby ass kicked for becoming what he was today.

He reached his cubicle, just in time to see the only office evidence of him and Laura crash from the wall to the floor. It hit his desk on the way down and the glass spider-webbed.

Sandy, his chubby cubicle partner, spun her chair. "Oh my God! Peter. I am so sorry." Pete picked up the picture and frame, testing the weight of it in his hands. "Let me get you some money for a new frame." Sandy wheeled back around and burrowed through the top drawer of her desk.

Pete looked closely at the picture, taken when they first got married, when Laura had that terrible perm and he had that terrible mustache. Had they been happy? Pete's smile seemed to be hanging on for dear life. It could have been the stuffy photo studio. Or the next-in-line crying infant. But Laura?

"All I have is a couple of ones—I hit the vending machine early today because they keep running out of Diet Cokes!—but hopefully this will help some. And I can bring some tomorrow, I guess."

Pete looked up from the picture to Sandy's hand, holding two crumpled bills. "Don't worry about it." He lifted the picture above his head and, after an exaggerated windup, tossed it in the small trashcan in the corner of his cubicle.

∞

At lunch, Pete liked to go somewhere for a club sandwich. Unless he went to Duffy's, then it was a Reuben. He tried to get out of the office. He liked the soft buzz of cafes, the hum of conversation. It was like falling asleep with the television on.

But today he needed a drink. "Fifteen eighty-four." The clerk behind the counter at the Shell station couldn't be any older than his son. Pete handed him a twenty. "Rough day, huh?" the clerk asked.

He took his four dollars and sixteen cents, his burrito, his tall boy of PBR, and his fifth of whiskey and headed for the park in the downtown business area: a couple of benches on a small section of grass that doubled as a breeding ground for Canadian geese.

Pete should have brought a loaf of bread. And another pair of shoes. As he tiptoed through the geese-shit landmines, he cracked the turn cap seal of the whiskey and poured himself a mouthful. He took a seat on one of the benches and slid the burrito from his jacket pocket. As usual, the edges were hot enough to scald his tongue, the center ice cold. Try your damnedest to do something right, Pete thought. Always a bit too much of one thing and a bit too little of another. Pete ate the burrito anyway, the beans in the center cooling the tip of his burnt tongue.

"You think I was gonna give the bad parts to you?" Pete shouted at the geese. He cracked open the PBR, chugged a bit down, and poured whiskey into the can. "I worked hard for that burrito—and you want me to just give it over to you? You're good for nothing mooches is what you are."

Blank stares from the gaggle. One goose honked back at him.

"Don't you talk back at me! You're nothing but a ..." A woman walked past on the sidewalk. She stared, mouth agape, at him, so he stared right back at her and finished berating the goose: "A goose-feathered whore." The woman picked up her pace.

Pete tipped the can back and followed one swallow with another until it was empty. He lay down on the bench, shielding his eyes from the sun with one arm and letting the other hang down, where he kept a tight grip on the whiskey. He could feel the combination of sun and booze and burrito working its way through his blood. He yawned and pulled himself halfway up for a couple more pulls on the bottle. He lay back down and in a blink completed his metamorphosis: a full-on bum, drunk and fast asleep on a park bench.

∞

Attn: Pete McConnell

Need to see you in my office right away.

—James T Reardon

Terse. Succinct. It did not bode well. Pete placed the bulk of his weight on the handles of his office chair and lifted himself out of the seat. As he stood, he neglected to transfer his weight to the front of his feet and the back wheels of the chair slipped from underneath him and crashed to the floor. Pete managed to catch himself on the cubicle wall.

"Are you okay, Pete?" Sally asked.

Pete wiped his shirtsleeve across his mouth, catching some loose saliva that had escaped through his teeth and dribbled down his bottom lip.

"Yeah. Fine. It's nice that you're so worried though." Pete pressed the front of his pant with the palm of his hands, trying to remove the wrinkles. "I'm fine for now anyway. Check back in a few. I'm about to get fired."

Sandy's face was caught somewhere between concern and disgust. She looked at his left hand. Pete followed her glance and realized he was still carrying a now-nearly empty bottle of whiskey. He fish-flopped his open hand at Sandy and brought the bottle to his mouth, and took the final slug.

"What's the saying? Don't let your right hand know what your left is doing?" He smiled and this time did not catch the saliva escaping from his mouth. It rolled out the left side of his mouth and down his stubbly face. "Wish me luck, baby!"
Sandy was petrified. "Good luck?"

Pete tossed the empty bottle on top of the broken frame and quoted his rookie ball manager:

"Luck is for sissies and idiots."

∞

"Mr. McConnell. I'm sure you know why I've called you in here."

Pete looked over the long desk in front of him. A deep cherry finish, shiny and polished, the opposite of his laminate metal-framed desk. The big golden plaque at the front of the desk read James T. Reardon III. Pete suddenly wished he was the third of something. It sounded important. Maybe he would start using a middle initial.

"Pete C. McConnell, sir." Was he slurring his words? "But you can call me Pete." He couldn't quite tell. The room was too bright. Pete stood up. "Mr. Reardon." He could hear the voice of his mother: *I'm gonna tan your rear.* She didn't believe in fowl language. Pete chuckled to himself. Mr. Assdon. "I'm sorry. Can I call you James? Maybe Jim?" Pete coughed out a laugh from the bottom of his throat. "Trey?" He felt like he was in church, his laugh creeping up from his feet.

"Is something funny, Mr. McConnell?" James Reardon III was halfway out of his chair, looking anxious about Pete's next step. He extended his arm and swept an open palm in the direction of the chairs in front of his desk, Vanna White introducing a puzzle. "Why don't you have a seat?"

"Something about your name. God, it's bright in here." Pete swept his hand towards the window and caught his wrist in the blinds. "How *does* Vanna do it?" Pete shielded his eyes. "Can I close these blinds? It's like playing ball in the afternoon. I could use some eye-black. The light's hitting me right in the eyes and my head's just throbbing."

"That's what I've called you in here for, Mr. McConnell."

"For eyeblack?" Pete patted down his pockets. "I'm sure I've got some in my bat bag. But I don't keep any at work."

"No, Mr. McConnell. Your headaches."

Pete squinted his eyes and scratched his scalp. A few white flakes fell onto his shirt. He brushed them off. "Oh. You got some aspirin or something for me? I'm all out of ibuprofen at home." Pete laughed again, short and staccato.

"Although, come to think of it, I should have checked the bat bag for that too."

Reardon arched an eyebrow and continued. "This company will not tolerate this kind of behavior, Mr. McConnell. We tried to overlook your falling efficiency, your propensity for tardiness—" Reardon raised his cheek bones, a smile of contempt "—your hygiene and your personal ... disarray. You've been a solid employee for a long—"

"An asset to the company. A *rear*et to the company." Pete laughed and clapped a hand over his mouth.

"Excuse me?"

"Nothing, your majesty, please go on. Please. A solid employee, yada, yada, yada."

"Yes, a solid employee. But, this Mr. McConnell—coming to work drunk—this will not do. It is totally unacceptable behavior."

Pete sat down. The chair was more comfortable than the loveseat. He leaned forward and reached his hands across the desk. "Now, Trey. Let's get one thing straight. I did not come to drunk work—" Pete bent his neck, pressing his chin to his clavicle. He belched. "I mean, work drunk."

"Excuse me?"

"First, stop excusing yourself. I'm the one with indigestion. Second, I didn't come to work drunk. I came back from lunch drunk."

Pete could not hold back any longer. He threw his head back and belly laughed, the kind of laugh he thought God must have sounded the day he created man. He fell out of the expensive wood and vinyl chair and, in an attempt to regain his standing, knocked his boss's pen holder—presented by the West Wind Country Club for his fifth place finish in last spring's fundraiser golf tournament—to the floor. Pete fell back over on the ground and continued to laugh.

"Get out of my office, Mr. McConnell. Get out of my office, get your things from your desk and do not come back. For work, for a visit, for anything. I will call security. Thank you for your time with the company."

∞

Pete stumbled his way back to his desk. Good riddance. He wouldn't miss anything about this job. Maybe Sally. She was nice. And Pete did not think he was the kind of guy to forget kindness. He passed a cubicle full of guys about his son's age, laughing, unaware of how wretched their lives were going to get. One of them turned up the speakers attached to his computer. The speakers buzzed, overloaded with low end from some rap song.

Pete reached his desk and grabbed an empty filing box. He threw a few things in—some good pens, a ream of paper, anything of value—and stood up, surveying the landscape of four-foot walls and factory-made desks. Three rows over and two cubicles up, the ringleader of the hip-hop cubicle was hooting. The kid's high-pitched laugh clashed with the fuzzy beat from the speakers. Pete watched as he flipped the open collar of his blue-with-white-pinstripes shirt and moved his feet in near-rhythm with the music. Pete tugged on the knot of his tie, loosening its grip on his neck. Open-collared shirts were against company policy.

Pete picked up his box and began his slow walk down the middle aisle of the office. The song stopped for a moment, only to be restarted. His head pounded to the distorted beat. He eyed the prep school thugs, cursing under his breath, focusing on the thin stripes of the blue and white shirt. A small tuft of hair rose up from the V of the open collar. At what age does a boy develop chest hair? He moved his eyes up the neck to the face, the mouth wide with laughter. Suddenly he was familiar, Pete knew the sheen of his white teeth. That morning, outside of Laura's apartment, the man, the boy, the stack of mail, the touch of the arm. The lingering. Here in his office, working here all the time, and him knowing nothing and this punk kid saying nothing.

The hairs on the back of his neck stood up. His fingers curled and uncurled. The heart inside in his chest pounded with gorilla fury, he was dreaming of landslides and earth-rending quakes, visions of mushroom clouds and Jean-Claude Van Damme movies. His insides were a steam engine, chugging and churning, tilling the crusted dirt that covered his heart, exposing the blood and the guts of a pre-industrial, pre-agricultural, pre-civilized man. That heart, malnourished by soft mattresses and strong drinks and TV dads, inkled the feeling of being alive, recalled the visceral act of beating thump-thump, thump-thump. It remembered tire swings over Charlie Creek, model cars stuffed with Black Cats, skinned knees and broken fingers.

"Hey guy? Can I get you to turn that down a little?"

The kid turned from his copy-machine cadre to face Pete: "Hey guy?" he mocked. "Can I get you to shut up?"

He turned back to his posse and Pete listened to the laughter crescendo. He tapped him on the shoulder. "What did you say your name was?"

The kid twisted his head ninety degrees, his body still facing away from Pete. "I didn't say." His lip curled into a cocky smile.

"I see. Well I'm Pete. And you are?"

He motioned at Pete's box, tipping his head back and pointing with his nose. "Why don't you take your shit and leave?"

Pete pushed air through his lips in an exaggerated sigh, a horse neigh. "The thing is, I have this nasty headache and your music just isn't helping things."

"I'm sorry Pete." Spit sprayed Pete's face at the hard consonant. "I missed that. Did you say you're hung over and you're a failure and your wife left you and you need a shoulder to cry on?"

Heads were beginning to appear over the tops of cubicle walls like a South Dakota prairie dog village.

Pete almost choked on his sharp inhale. The open collar. The pinstriped shirt. The rap music. "Did you say something about my wife?"

Pete, the modern man, did not believe in beating his wife into submission to make her stay. That did not mean he didn't believe in beating Caveman B.

Pete's right fist met the center of the kid's face, his knuckles bowing the nose like a wishbone, the accompanying soundtrack a sick *crack*.

The kid cupped his hands over his nose, blood running down through his fingers, a steady stream pouring from his fingers. The blood had just reached the kid's chin when Pete's left fist hooked across his body, slamming into the jawbone.

The kid crumpled to the floor.

Pete shook the tingle from his hand and wished for a caveman beating stick.

A gasp. A woman two rows over fainted. The distorted beat continued to bounce. Pete kicked the kid in the ribs, his loafer pounding into that pinstriped shirt, in rhythm with the fuzzy speakers. One of the posse members piped up, "Jesus, man. You're sick," before turning to address the rest of the office, all the heads with cubicles for bodies. "Somebody call security."

Though Pete wore more fat than muscle now and more skin than hair and he sea-swayed with booze, no one in the office would have called him old or drunk or weak or washed up. It was a transfiguration: the flabby and flaccid replaced, the fluorescent lights spotlighting him like a holy beam, as he stood over the moaning body in the middle of the office.

Pete stepped over the moaning lump and into the cubicle and shut off the speakers. He looked around the office at the faces, horrified, stupefied, some of them smiling. He wiped his bloody knuckles on his yellowish-white Oxford shirt and headed for the exit.

∞

Pete woke up, his forehead red where it was pressed against the steering wheel. He wiped the sleeve of his shirt across his mouth, his excess saliva mixing with the small specks of blood left on the back of his hand. He wrung his hands over the steering wheel, trying to get his bearings. He turned

the key, already in the ignition. The engine fired
and the dash lit up, the clock read 3:05. Laura
would be packing up her canvas bags, preparing to
leave school. He watched her in his mind, brushing
her hair out of her eyes, teasing her bangs, ironing
out the front of her skirt with the palms of her
hands. Once a beauty queen, always a beauty queen.

   Pete looked in the rearview. Flecks of blood
freckled his face. He ran a rough hand through his
thick beard—when had he last shaved? He couldn't
remember. He would go home. Clean up. Swing by
and see her. Say sorry. Compliment. You pretty, me
sorry. Beat his chest, win her back.

Shoot The Lights Out

Luke Hawley   Joe Mann

Shoot The Lights Out

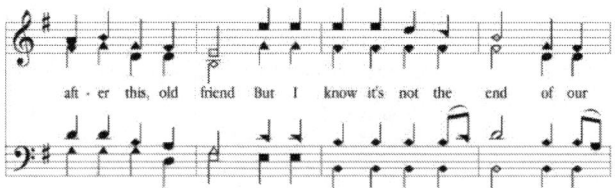

aft - er this, old friend But I know it's not the end of our

time. I can't tell you how I know, I don't have a lick of

proof, But I know it in my heart I do, I do.

Tomato Soup

"There's a Ray Bradbury short story—I can't think of what book it's in. The Pedestrian. That's the name of the story anyway. This guy gets picked up by the police one night—this is in the future of course—for not watching his television. He just wants to go for a walk, get out in the air. But it's illegal to do. You're supposed to stay home and watch television, I guess."

Moses listened to his old friend talk. The air was cooling. It was September, but a stubborn summer had stuck around keeping the leaves on the trees and the days hot and humid. He could smell it in the air though. Winter was coming. Autumn would pass in a blink, he'd wake up one morning to frost and all the leaves suddenly brown and scattered about his yard.

"That's why I followed John Prine's advice," Moses said.

"And what's that?" Roger was an avid reader but, having gone deaf in his left ear as a kid, never paid much attention to music.

"You know that old song. I can't think of the name." Moses warbled the best he could. "Blow up your TV ... something something ... grow a bunch of peaches ... something ... find Jesus."

Roger nodded slowly, "Quite a rendition." He put his hand over his eyes like a visor and looked at the streetlight on the boulevard.

"Of course, I didn't blow it up. It just quit and I never got a new one." Moses pushed his glasses up the bridge of his nose and looked up past the streetlight into the darkness of the sky. "I always wanted to take the parts out and turn it into a fish bowl."

"You should."

"Yeah." Moses stretched his arms over his head. "I'm too old for that."

They both laughed, pitched low and full of gravel, quiet laughs laid underneath the treble of cicadas and crickets. In the distance, a semi downshifted, jake-braking its way down the slope on the western edge of town.

"I think my brain's going, Rog." Moses ran his hands through the hair on the sides of his head. When his hands reached the back of his head, he made two fists and pulled the hair into his fingers. It was strange to have thick hair around his head and no hair on the top.

"Can't be." Roger locked his fingers, bent them backwards and cracked them against his chin. "If you think it's going, then you still have it enough to know something at all."

"Makes sense." Moses nodded. "Sure is good to have smart friends."

"Dad!" Roger's daughter, Erica, hollered from the front door. "Dad! Can you please come inside?"

Without turning his head: "No dear, I cannot."

"Please Dad. Nobody likes a creeper. Come on in and watch some television."

Smiling so only Moses could see: "Absolutely not."

"Or read one of your books."

"Later, Honey." Roger raised his hand over his head and flopped it back and forth, a fish on a stringer. "I'm talking with my old friend here. I'll come in later." The door shut, echoing a metallic clang. "Speaking of losing your mind."

Moses hmphed. "Is she pregnant?"

"She thinks I'm losing mine. Because I don't like television." Roger stared into the dark sky, trying to measure the space between the stars. "Because I sit out here. So they're gonna send me away."

"Say what now?"

"I saw the paperwork on the counter. Ebenezer, I guess, over on the south side of town."

"That fancy new place?"

"They can dress it up as much as they want. I can see the razor wire."

"When are they taking you?"

Roger twisted his mouth, most of his lips moving in the direction of his right nostril. "Don't know."

"It wasn't supposed to go this way." Moses thought of his wife, dead seven years. "Every almanac I've ever laid eyes on said we were supposed to be the first to go. I feel like an old prune, dried up and unwanted."

"Now that's not quite right," Roger said, holding up his hand, pointing like a politician. "Plenty of people want prunes."

"Just old people." Moses chuckled. "Babies too, I guess."

"I read a blurb about Bradbury the other day. Said when he died, he wanted to be cremated and he wanted his ashes put in a Campbell's Tomato Soup can and sent on a rocket to Mars."

Moses raised his shaggy white eyebrows. "Better to burn up than dry up, I suppose."

"His Mars obsession," Roger noted. "Must love tomato soup too. Just put one and the other together."

"I'll be damned."

"Thing is, Moses, I don't love anything that much. I don't love anything as much as Ray Bradbury loves tomato soup."

Moses shifted in his chair. They were old lawn chairs, the kind with the plasticky straps woven together. Every time he shifted, the chair tried to fold in on him. He preferred a good wooden chair, a rocker if he could. Plenty hanging in the shop, but they didn't fold up for the back of the truck. Ease over comfort, he thought: Aren't those two supposed to go hand in hand?

They were quiet then, for a long time, feeling the cool come down like a damp towel, listening to the buzz of the streetlamp.

"I hate that thing," Roger said.

"What thing?"

"That light." Roger pointed to the corner. "Blocks out most of the stars. And buzzes to beat the band."

Moses squinted his eyes and looked at the light, then at the sky. "Seems pretty full of stars to me."

"You can't even see the half of them." Roger stood up and began to search the ground around his chair. "Help me find a rock, Moses."

Moses stood up and looked around the boulevard. "You think it's plastic?"

"What?" Roger got down on his hands and knees.

"The light cover. I bet it's plastic. I bet we'll hit it and those rocks'll just come flying back at us." Moses put his hand up over his eyes. Now that he was looking at it, it did seem awfully bright. A world full of people scared of the dark; he was too old for that nonsense now. "Hold on then, Rog. Let me check my truck."

Roger continued to search the ground and Moses walked around the lawn chair to the driveway. They had been sitting a long time, longer than usual, and he could feel the extra air in his joints. He high stepped and his hips popped, followed by his knees, his ankles, and down through his toes. Moses thought about what Roger said, about the nursing home, and he knew he wouldn't go like that. He would go rocketing out into the dark.

He pulled his toolbox from the bed and found two long, thick nails, the kind he used making picnic tables. He grabbed a couple of short tow straps and one long one and walked back over to sit in the chair.

"Find a good rock?" Moses asked.

"No. But I might walk around back." Roger stood and dusted off the knees of his slacks. "I think the peonies back there are planted in rock beds."

"Just hold on. I'm gonna need your help. Hold this." He handed Roger a nail and a short strap and sat back in the lawn chair. He lifted his left boot up on his right knee and held the nail along the inside of the boot, the sharp edge an inch or so past the sole. He wrapped the short tow strap around his ankle and ratcheted the nail tight against his boot. He took the nail and the short strap from Roger and repeated the action on his right boot. "You're gonna have to help me over there. It's tough to walk in pole spikes."

"You've done this before?" Roger took Moses by the elbow and lifted him out of the chair.

Moses read the worry in Roger's face. "When we were kids, my brothers and I would shimmy up skinny little aspens and jump from tree to tree, like a bunch of howler monkeys. Lord knows I can't shimmy anymore." He chinned at his boots. "This ought to help though."

They stood underneath the streetlight looking up at the yellow-orange glow. Moses looked past Roger down the block. "Go grab a hammer from the truck, would you?" Roger nodded and Moses staked his right boot into the meat of the pole. The nail dug into the bulbous bone on the inside of his ankle. He placed the long strap around the pole and grunted, heaving up his left foot, to where he was off the ground. He leaned back and let the tow strap hold his weight.

"Here you go." Roger was back with the hammer. "Are you sure about this?"

"Hook it in my belt." Moses shifted his weight towards Roger. "I'm as sure about this as I am about anything anymore. You should be asking, 'Are you sure about you?', in reference to my body. That I am not sure about. But"—Moses took another step, holding tight to the tow strap—"I sure as hell am not going to just dry up and die. Just dying sounds like about the worst thing I can imagine."

"So you're okay breaking your neck for a light bulb?"

"It's something, ain't it? For stars I can't see?" With each step, Moses grunted louder, feeling the sweat forming on his leather skin. The grunts and sweat were the same as when he worked in the shop, sanding chairs and hammering tables. But the blood pumping to his temples was something different, like the difference between making something comfortable to sit on and swinging a hammer in the name of destruction. "Who knows, maybe all those extra stars will be my tomato soup."

Halfway up the pole he thought he was having a heart attack and he stopped for a moment. "Are you alright?" whispered-shouted Roger. Moses wanted to wipe the sweat off of his forehead, but he couldn't let go of the tow strap. He grunted again and took the final steps to the top of the light.

"Is it plastic?"

Moses steadied himself against the pole, leaning into it and put all his weight on the spikes of his boots. He hugged the pole with one arm and with his other hand pulled at one side of the covering, bending it slightly, slipping it out of its hold. He looked down at Roger and dropped the cover to the right of him. It bounced off the boulevard and clanged into the street, sounding like a bucket of spilled soup cans.

"Are you ready?" He could see Roger nodding, smiling, lit like a halo by the brightness of the uncovered bulb. There was something maniacal about him, in the way he rubbed his hands together, close to his chest. With his free hand, Moses pulled the hammer from his belt and swung at the light bulb, covering his face with his swinging arm. Through squinted eyes he saw the explosion, the burst of brightness followed by the sound of glass hitting the pavement of the street. He looked down at Roger, standing off to one side of the pole, staring up past him. Moses followed his old friend's gaze, looking up into the night, into the stars, into the millions of tiny lights set against the black backdrop of darkness.

Contributors

Holly Neeley lives in Russelville, Arkansas with her husband, Jon, and her two sweet kids: Leeland and Olive. When she's not elbow deep in the work of mothering, she freelances as an artist and photographer. You can find her work on Facebook at Holly Neeley Photography.

Joe Mann is a web professional who also holds a masters degree in music history from the University of Nebraska. Joe resides in St. Paul, Minnesota with his pet fish, Wanda.

Paul Dudrey is a composer with degrees in music education and classical composition. Paul lives and works in Portland, Oregon (where good art still flourishes and the inspiration of God's green Earth is close at hand) with his wife Kacy, daughter Annabelle, and their two dogs. His music can be found at www.pauldudrey.com

Acknowledgements

Where to start? Sarah: For your unwavering belief in all my shifting dreams. *I could be your one man band and you could be my steady hand.* And Eden and Judah, who will probably have no memory of this process, but have given me the best editing breaks known to humankind, as well as a surprising amount of naptime for me to write. To the rest of my family: thanks for always telling stories and for letting me steal some of yours.

Diane: Oh my goodness. I couldn't have asked for a more patient and kind and generous publisher. You're a hero of mine and I hope if I ever retire that I can achieve a fraction of what you are doing now.

Joe: Thanks for inviting me to the River Otter family. And for all the editing.

Tim: Remember when you caught that single period that was accidentally bolded? I'll never forget it. Thank you for being so focused. And excellent.

To my mentors—Fred Arroyo, Kate Gale, Pope Brock, and Patricia Lear—thanks for unleashing me. And for teaching me that it's important to be funny (or at least try) and that revision, however painful, is crucial. And for showing me how to live as a writer.

Josh: The record sounds incredible--I didn't know if the songs would ever sound like I wanted them to, but they do, and that's thanks to you. And for the rest of the (free) elbow grease: Thank you.

Holly: For the design. And the last minute nature of it.

Paul and Joe: The hymns were a whim (and a rhyme?). They turned out—I was going to use a superlative, but what I'd like to say is: They're perfect.

And to anyone who might read these stories. Thank you for taking the time. Even though they're short stories, I understand the limited nature of time and I appreciate that you took a sliver of your life and joined me in my fake one.

Reprint Permission

The Smell of Burning Leaves was first published online by the fine people at sleetmagazine.com in the Fall 2011 edition.

Painting Elephants was first published in the award-winning journal *Grey Sparrow* in the Fall 2011 edition.

Almond Bark was first published by *Hobart Literary Journal* in December of 2010. It also won the short story competition at *Wild Violet Journal*.

Tomato Soup was first published in the November 2011 edition of *The Blotter*.

Quotation, "Music was my refuge. I could crawl into the space between my notes and curl my back to loneliness." reprinted from *Gather Together in My Name*, by Maya Angelou, Mass Market Paperback Publishing.

Luke Hawley lives in the cold of Minnesota with his wife and two small kids. He spends his time writing, growing a beard, and building bookcases out of old windows. This is his first book.

∞

Songs for *The Northwoods Hymnal* are available at **www.lhawley.com.** You will need to enter this password: **elephantheart**

21828209R00124

Made in the USA
Middletown, DE
12 July 2015